I Love to Read!

READ TODAY
for a better tomorrow
www.njread2kids.org
New Jersey Department of Education

THIS BOOK BELONGS TO:

THE LITTLE BIG BOOK *for*

GIRLS

Edited by
ALICE WONG & LENA TABORI

Designed by
TIMOTHY SHANER & CHRISTOPHER MEASOM

welcome
BOOKS
NEW YORK • SAN FRANCISCO

Published in 2003 by Welcome Books® • An imprint of Welcome Enterprises, Inc.
6 West 18 Street, New York, NY 10011 • (212) 989-3200; Fax (212) 989-3205
e-mail: info@welcomebooks.biz • www.welcomebooks.biz

Publisher: Lena Tabori   *Project Director:* Alice Wong
Designers: Timothy Shaner and Christopher Measom
Project Assistants: Jacinta O'Halloran, Lawrence Chesler, and Nicholas Liu
Activities and Recipes by Monique Peterson   *Heroines text by* David Cashion
Introductions to literary excerpts by Sara Baysinger
Additional text by Sara Baysinger, Rachel Hertz, and Deidra Garcia
Production Assitants: Kate Shaw and Naomi Irie   *Activities line illustrations by* Lawrence Chesler
Front jacket illustration by Ann Brockman

Distributed to the trade in the U.S. and Canada by Andrews McMeel Distribution Services
Order Department and Customer Service (800) 943-9839 Orders Only Fax (800) 943-9831

LIBRARY OF CONGRESS CATALOGING-IN-PUBLICATION DATA
The little big book for girls / edited by Alice Wong and Lena Tabori.
    p.cm. – (The Little big book series)
    Summary: An illustrated collection of literary excerpts, poems, songs, games,
recipes, miscellaneous facts, and activities for girls.
    ISBN 0-941807-81-9
    1. Girls—Literary collections. [1. Girls—Literary collections.] 1. Wong, Alice.
II. Tabori, Lena. III. Little big book (New York, N.Y.)
PZ5.L6863 2003
808.8'0083'42—dc21
                                                                            2002193397

Printed in Singapore
FIRST EDITION
1 3 5 7 9 10 8 6 4 2

Contents

Activities

Poetry

Contents

Contents

Welcome

Welcome girls, **welcome!**
You're in for a special treat.
This book is filled with the coolest stuff
To read, to do, to eat!

So come meet **Little Women**
And a girl named Heidi, too.
Ponder life with Margaret
You'll find she's a lot like you.

Travel with Alice to Wonderland
And **visit Sunnybrook Farm**,
Get lost in The Secret Garden—
It's filled with mystery and charm.

Take a ride with Velvet
And snoop with Harriet the Spy,
Laugh along with Pippi—
She sure can spin a lie!

Tell a joke or spooky tale,
    Eat a chewy Cinnamon Snail.
Play a card game like Go Fish,
    Bake a cake or make a wish.

    Braid, weave, *rhyme and sing*,
        Fashion a 3-way decoder ring.
    Write a note with invisible ink,
        Brew a Very Berry drink!

        Recite a poem or read a palm,
            Learn to sew just like your mom.
        Discover women who paved the way,
            Dream of who you'll become one day.

Welcome girls, welcome!
    You are special, *it is true*.
That's why we decided
    To make a book that's *just for you!*

Laura Ingalls Wilder published nine books in her beloved Little House series. *Little House in the Big Woods* (1932) was the first in the series and presents American frontier life through a child's eyes. The Ingalls' family story begins in 1871. Four-year-old Laura lives in a little log cabin on the edge of the Big Woods of Wisconsin with her Pa, her Ma, her sisters Mary and Carrie, and their loyal dog, Jack. The rugged pioneer life is at times trying for the family. Facing many adversities, they work hard to grow and find their own food in preparation for the long, cold winters. The girls learn to be self-sufficient as they help their mother with the traditional household chores. But despite the hard work, life proves to be exciting and engaging for Laura. The family radiates warmth and maintains strong traditions—a favorite being Pa's bedtime stories and songs.

Laura and Mary helped Ma with the work. Every morning there were the dishes to wipe. Mary wiped more of them than Laura because she was bigger, but Laura always wiped carefully her own little cup and plate.

By the time the dishes were all wiped and set away, the trundle bed was aired. Then, standing one on each side, Laura and Mary straightened the covers, tucked them in well at the foot and the sides, plumped up the pillows and put them in place. Then Ma pushed the trundle bed into its place under the big bed.

After this was done, Ma began the work that belonged to that day. Each day had its own proper work. Ma used to say:

"Wash on Monday,
Iron on Tuesday,
Mend on Wednesday,
Churn on Thursday,
Clean on Friday,
Bake on Saturday,
Rest on Sunday."

Laura liked the churning and the baking days best of all the week.

In winter the cream was not yellow as it was in summer, and butter churned from it was white and not so pretty. Ma liked everything on her table to be pretty, so in the wintertime she colored the butter.

Little House in the Big Woods

by Laura Ingalls Wilder

After she had put the cream in the tall crockery churn and set it near the stove to warm, she washed and scraped a long orange-colored carrot. Then she grated it on the bottom of the old, leaky tin pan that Pa had punched full of nail-holes for her. Ma rubbed the carrot across the roughness until she had rubbed it all through the holes, and when she lifted up the pan, there was a soft, juicy mound of grated carrot.

Laura liked the churning and the baking days best of all the week.

She put this in a little pan of milk on the stove and when the milk was hot she poured milk and carrot into a cloth bag. Then she squeezed the bright yellow milk into the churn, where it colored all the cream. Now the butter would be yellow.

Laura and Mary were allowed to eat the carrot after the milk had been squeezed out. Mary thought she ought to have the larger share because she was older, and Laura said she should have it because she was littler. But Ma said they must divide it evenly. It was very good.

When the cream was ready, Ma scalded the long wooden churn dash, put it in the churn, and dropped the wooden churn-cover over it. The churn cover had a little round hold in the middle, and Ma moved the dash up and down, up and down, through the hole.

She churned for a long time. Mary could sometimes churn while Ma rested, but the dash was too heavy for Laura.

At first the splashes of cream showed thick and smooth around the little hole. After a long time, they began to look grainy. Then Ma churned more slowly, and on the dash there began to appear tiny grains of yellow butter.

When Ma took off the churn cover, there was the butter in a golden lump, drowning in the buttermilk. Then Ma took out the lump with a wooden paddle, into a wooden bowl, and she washed it many times in cold water, turning it over and over and working it with the paddle until the water ran clear. After that she salted it.

Now came the best part of the churning. Ma molded the butter. On the loose bottom of the wooden butter mold was carved the picture of a strawberry with two strawberry leaves.

With the paddle Ma packed butter tightly into the mold until it was full. Then she turned it upside down over a plate, and pushed on the handle of the loose bottom. The little, firm pat of golden butter came out, with the strawberry and its leaves molded on the top.

Laura and Mary watched, breathless, one on each side of Ma, while the golden little butter pats, each with its strawberry on the top, dropped onto the plate as Ma put all the butter through the mold. Then Ma gave them each a drink of good, fresh buttermilk.

On Saturdays, when Ma made the bread, they each had a little piece of dough to make into a little loaf. They might have a bit of cookie dough too, to make little cookies, and once Laura even made a pie in the patty-pan.

After the day's work was done, Ma sometimes cut paper dolls for them. She cut the dolls out of stiff white paper, and drew the faces with a pencil. Then from bits of colored paper she cut dresses and hats, ribbons and laces, so that Laura and Mary could dress their dolls beautifully.

But the best time of all was at night, when Pa came home.

He would come in from his tramping through the snowy woods with tiny icicles hanging on the ends of his mustaches. He would hang his gun on the wall over the door, throw off his fur cap and coat and mittens, and call: "Where's my little half-pint of sweet cider half drunk up?"

That was Laura, because she was so small.

Laura and Mary would run to climb on his knees and sit there while he warmed himself by the fire. Then he would put on his coat and cap and mittens again and go out to do the chores and bring in plenty of wood for the fire.

Sometimes, when Pa had walked his traplines quickly because the traps were empty, or when he had got some game sooner than usual, he would come home early. Then he would have time to play with Laura and Mary.

One game they loved was called mad dog. Pa would run his fingers through his thick, brown hair, standing it all up on end. Then he dropped on all fours and, growling, he chased Laura and Mary all around the room, trying to get them cornered where they couldn't get away.

They were quick at dodging and running, but once he caught them against the wood box, behind the stove. They couldn't get past Pa, and there was no other way out.

Then Pa growled so terribly, his hair was so wild and his eyes so fierce that it all seemed real. Mary was so frightened that she could not move. But as Pa came nearer Laura screamed, and with a wild leap and a scramble she went over the wood box, dragging Mary with her.

And at once there was no mad dog at all. There was only Pa standing there with his blue eyes shining, looking at Laura.

"Well!" he said to her. "You're only a little half-pint of cider half drunk up, but by Jinks! you're as strong as a little French horse!"

"You shouldn't frighten the children so, Charles," Ma said. "Look how big their eyes are."

Pa looked, and then he took down his fiddle. He began to play and sing.

"Yankee Doodle went to town,
He wore his striped trousies,
He swore he couldn't see the town,
There was so many houses."

Laura and Mary forgot all about the mad dog.

"And there he saw some great big guns,
Big as a log of maple,
And every time they turned 'em round,
It took two yoke of cattle.

"And every time they fired 'em off,
It took a horn of power,
It made a noise like father's gun,
Only a nation louder."

But the best time of all was at night, when Pa came home.

Pa was keeping time with his foot, and Laura clapped her hands to the music when he sang,

"And I'll sing Yankee Doodle-de-do,
And I'll sing Yankee Doodle,
And I'll sing Yankee Doodle-de-do,
And I'll sing Yankee Doodle!"

All alone in the wild Big Woods, and the snow, and the cold, the little log house was warm and snug and cosy. Pa and Ma and Mary and Laura and Baby Carrie were comfortable and happy there, especially at night.

19

For the best muffin recipe ever, try these strawberry corn muffins. The yogurt keeps them moist and the fresh strawberries gives them something extra tasty in every bite. Take the nip out of a frosty morning with hot, creamy oatmeal—you'll be glowing from head to toe all day long! *Parfait* means "perfect" in French, which is a fitting name for these fruity treats that are just as good for dessert as they are for breakfast. For simpler cooking, cinnamon snails and toast can both be made in the toaster oven.

Good Morning!

Strawberry Corn Muffins

12 baking cups
1/2 cup fresh strawberries, chopped
5 tablespoons sugar
1 cup yellow cornmeal
1 cup flour
1 tablespoon baking powder
1 extra-large egg
8 ounces strawberry yogurt
3 tablespoons vegetable oil
1 teaspoon baking soda
1 teaspoon vanilla

1. Line a muffin tin with baking cups and pre-heat oven to 400°F.
2. In a glass measuring cup, toss strawberries with 1 tablespoon sugar.
3. In a large bowl, mix cornmeal, flour, baking powder, and remaining sugar.
4. In a small bowl, beat together egg, yogurt, oil, baking soda, and vanilla. Blend in strawberries.
5. Use a wooden spoon to stir the wet ingredients into the flour mixture. Blend together until all of the flour is moistened.
6. Spoon batter into muffin cups. Bake for 15 minutes, or until tops spring back when lightly pressed.

Makes 12 muffins.

Some Like it Hot: Creamy Oatmeal

3 cups milk
1 1/2 cups rolled oats

1. In a saucepan, stir oats into milk and cook over medium heat until milk starts to bubble.
2. Continue to stir frequently over low heat for about 5 minutes, until oatmeal begins to thicken. Remove from heat.
3. Ladle into bowls and serve hot with one of several toppings: chopped walnuts, banana slices, brown sugar, raisins, peach slices, honey, cinnamon apple slices, cranberries, raspberry syrup, blueberries, maple syrup.

Makes 2 to 3 servings.

Fruity Breakfast Parfaits

BLUEBERRY PEACH

2 cups fresh blueberries
1/2 cup peach jam
2 cups vanilla or lemon yogurt
1/2 cup toasted almonds, sliced

1. In a microwavable bowl, combine blueberries and jam. Microwave on high for 2 to 3 minutes or until berries are soft. Allow berries to cool to room temperature.
2. In four sundae glasses, layer a few tablespoons of yogurt, blueberry sauce, and a sprinkling of almonds. Repeat for two to three more layers.

Makes 4 servings.

CHOCO-BERRY CRUNCH

2 cups raspberries
1 tablespoon sugar
2 cups vanilla yogurt
2 tablespoons cocoa powder
1/2 cup granola

1. In a small bowl, mix raspberries and sugar.
2. In a separate bowl, mix yogurt and cocoa powder.
3. In four sundae glasses, add a few tablespoons of the yogurt mixture, followed by a few tablespoons of raspberries. Sprinkle a layer of granola on top. Repeat for three more layers. Chill until ready to serve.

Makes 4 servings.

Cinnamon Snails

1/2 stick (1/4 cup) butter
2 tablespoons cinnamon
4 tablespoons sugar
6 bread slices with crusts removed
3 ounces whipped cream cheese, softened to room temperature

1. Preheat oven to 350°F. Line a cookie sheet with aluminum foil.
2. Put butter in small microwavable bowl and melt in microwave on high for about 2 minutes.
3. In a separate bowl, mix cinnamon and sugar until blended.
4. Use a rolling pin to flatten bread slices.
5. With a butter knife, spread a thin layer of cream cheese on flattened slices.
6. Roll up bread slices and seal the seams with extra cream cheese if necessary.
7. To make "snails," cut each roll into three or four sections.
8. Dip each snail into the melted butter and then into the cinnamon and sugar mixture until well coated.
9. Place snails on a cookie sheet and bake for 8 to 12 minutes, or until lightly browned and crispy.

Makes 18 to 24 snails.

French Toast Fingers

6 thick slices of day-old bread
3 large eggs
3/4 cup milk
1 teaspoon vanilla
1/2 teaspoon cinnamon
1/4 teaspoon nutmeg
2 teaspoons sugar

1. Remove the tray from a toaster oven and cover with aluminum foil. Set aside.
2. Cut bread slices into 2-inch-wide strips, or "fingers."
3. Whisk eggs in a bowl until blended. Mix in milk, vanilla, cinnamon, nutmeg, and sugar. Pour egg mixture into a shallow pan or dish.
4. Soak bread fingers in egg mixture.
5. Set toaster oven to broil.
6. Put a row of soaked bread fingers onto the foil-covered tray and broil for three minutes.
7. Using oven mitts and a spatula, carefully turn the fingers over and broil for another three minutes.
8. Remove toaster oven tray and dish fingers onto plates.
9. Repeat steps 6 through 8 until all fingers are toasted. Serve warm with maple syrup.

Makes 4 servings.

Three Little Birds

by Bob Marley

Don't worry
about a thing.
'Cause every
little thing's
gonna be
alright

Don't worry about a thing
Cause every little thing's gonna be alright
Singin' don't worry about a thing
Cause every little thing is gonna be alright

Rise up this mornin'
Smile with the rising sun
Three little birds
Pitch by my door step
Singin' sweet songs
Of melodies pure and true
Sayin', this is my message to you:

Don't worry about a thing
Cause every little thing is gonna be alright
Don't worry about a thing
Every little thing is gonna be alright

Then Laugh

by Bertha Adams Backus

Build for yourself a strong box,

Fashion each part with care;
When it's strong as your hand can make it,
Put all your troubles there;
Hide there all thought of your failures,
And each bitter cup that you quaff;
Lock all your heartaches within it,
Then sit on the lid and laugh.

Tell no one else its contents,
Never its secrets share;
When you've dropped in your care and worry
Keep them forever there;
Hide them from sight so completely
That the world will never dream half;
Fasten the strong box securely—

Then sit on the lid and laugh.

Tongue Twisters

Swan swam over the sea. Swim, swan, swim!
Swan swam back again. Well swum, swan!

How much wood would a woodchuck chuck
If a woodchuck could chuck wood?
He would chuck, he would, as much as he could,
And chuck as much wood as a woodchuck would
If a woodchuck could chuck wood.

You've no need to light a night-light
On a light night like tonight,
For a night-light's light's a slight light,
And tonight's a night that's light.
When a night's light, like tonight's light,
It is really not quite right
To light night-lights with their slight lights
On a light night like tonight.

Susan shineth
shoes and socks;
Socks and
shoes shines
Susan. She
ceased
shining
shoes and socks,
For shoes and socks
shock Susan.

Treasure Boxes

*Y*ou can be sure that Cleopatra and the Queen of Sheba kept their favorite gems hidden in a special spot. Even if you don't have a collection of diamonds, rubies, and emeralds, you can take a tip from royalty and design your own treasure boxes. Big or small, you can make them just the right size to store your trinkets, jewelry, and keepsakes.

*F*irst find a good container. Many cardboard boxes with lids work well, such as shoeboxes or oatmeal boxes. Large tea tins and cigar boxes are good for storing things, too. Collect smaller containers, such as matchboxes, peppermint tins, or film canisters, that can fit inside your big box. Give your box a soft touch—line it with felt or a scrap of special fabric such as velvet or brocade.

Collage Box

Magazines, postcards, stickers, stamps, scissors, glue

1. Find fun images in magazines and postcards. Cut them up to create a collage.
2. Glue overlapping images in place all over your box. Add stickers and stamps after the glue has dried.

Jeweled Box

Ruler, scissors, paper bag, glue, paste, ribbon, lace, buttons, sequins, rhinestones

1. Measure and cut strips of brown paper bag to fit on the sides and lid of your box. Glue them in place and let dry.
2. Use paste to cover the sides of your box with ribbon or lace.
3. Arrange buttons, sequins, and rhinestones in fun patterns and glue them on.

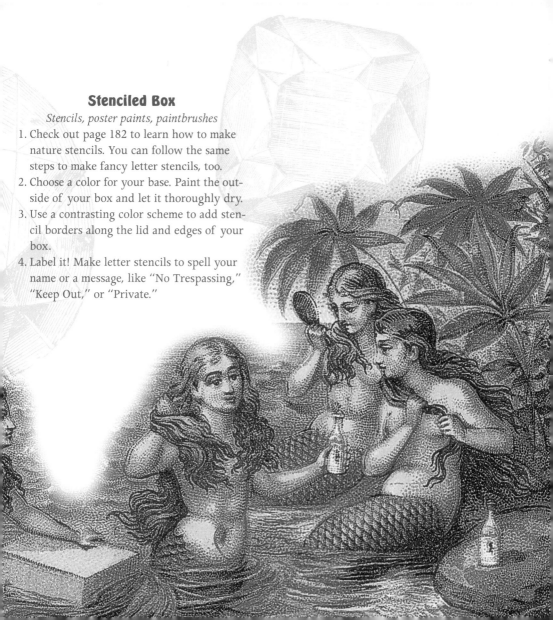

Stenciled Box

Stencils, poster paints, paintbrushes

1. Check out page 182 to learn how to make
   nature stencils. You can follow the same
   steps to make fancy letter stencils, too.
2. Choose a color for your base. Paint the outside of your box and let it thoroughly dry.
3. Use a contrasting color scheme to add stencil borders along the lid and edges of your
   box.
4. Label it! Make letter stencils to spell your
   name or a message, like "No Trespassing,"
   "Keep Out," or "Private."

Young Achievers

YOUNGEST DANCER

Winning the Junior World Line Dance
Championship in Nashville, TN, in January
1998, young blood SIOBHAN DUNN was
the world's youngest ever line-dance
champion at the age of 6 years, 6 months,
and 11 days.

YOUNGEST FLYER

KATRINA MUMAW had always wanted to
become a pilot. When she was 5, she
flew in her first air show, piloting a 1929
open-cockpit plane. Having already flown
everything from a Goodyear blimp to a
Russian Mig jet, she made history on July
12, 1994, when she flew a Mig jet at a
speed exceeding Mach 1.3—over 940
miles per hour—becoming the
youngest person, at the age of 11,

to break the sound barrier. Recently, after fourteen years of effort, she was accepted into the U.S. Air Force Academy in Colorado Springs, CO, where she will begin training in the class of 2006.

YOUNGEST RECIPIENT OF OSCAR/YOUNGEST SELF-MADE MILLIONAIRESS

On February 27, 1935, about six weeks shy of her 7th birthday, SHIRLEY TEMPLE won the Special Juvenile Award from the Academy of Motion Picture Arts and Sciences—the same year she became the youngest person to reach No. 1 at the box office. Later, in 1938, she became the youngest self-made millionairess.

YOUNGEST OSCAR WINNER

The youngest Oscar winner in Academy history is TATUM O'NEAL (USA) who won Best Supporting Actress for her role in *Paper Moon* (USA, 1973) on April 2, 1974. She was 10 years, 148 days old.

YOUNGEST "RECORDER"

It was said that MURASAKI SHIKIBU had such a remarkable memory that when she was 2 years old, she could already repeat a thousand lines of poetry after hearing them once.

YOUNGEST SINGER

ARETHA FRANKLIN started singing as a child at her father's church in Memphis. In 1956, she had already released her first album, *The Gospel Sound of Aretha Franklin*. She was 14 years old.

YOUNGEST WRITER

Famous for her classical poetry in the nineteenth century, ELIZABETH BARRETT BROWNING (1806–1861) could write verse by the time she was 4, and by 10 years of age had read the histories of Rome and England and the entire works of Shakespeare. She wrote her first "epic" poem when she was 11. The rhyming couplets spanned more than four books.

Do not stop thinking of life as an adventure. You have no security unless you can live bravely, excitingly, imaginatively.

—ELEANOR ROOSEVELT

The *Alice* books, which include *Alice's Adventures in Wonderland* and *Through the Looking-Glass*, are among the most famous and beloved children's stories in the English language. Charles Lutwidge Dodgson (1832–1898) wrote them in the mid-1800s under a pseudonym, Lewis Carroll. The inspiration for his whimsical stories about a young girl in a dream world was one Miss Alice Liddell, the daughter of the dean of Christ Church where Dodgson taught mathematics. Alice was four years old when she made the acquaintance of the reluctant author. She and her siblings, Lorina, Harry, and Edith, often went rowing with Mr. Dodgson where he would delight them with tales of Alice's adventures in Wonderland. It was on one of these trips that Alice asked Dodgson to write down these stories for her. Little did she know that this request would secure her immortality. As her story opens, we see a restless Alice sitting on the water's edge with her sister. When the white rabbit in his waistcoat runs by mumbling to himself, Alice's curiosity sends her scurrying after it. This is just the first in a series of many "out-of-the-way things" that Alice experiences. And so her adventures begin.

Alice was beginning to get very tired of sitting by her sister on the bank, and of having nothing to do: once or twice she had peeped into the book her sister was reading, but it had no pictures or conversations in it, "and what is the use of a book," thought Alice, "without pictures or conversations?"

So she was considering in her own mind (as well as she could, for the hot day made her feel very sleepy and stupid), whether the pleasure of making a daisy-chain would be worth the trouble of getting up and picking the daisies, when suddenly a White Rabbit with pink eyes ran close by her.

There was nothing so *very* remarkable in that; nor did Alice think it so very much out of the way to hear the Rabbit say to itself "Oh dear! Oh dear! I shall be too late!" (when she thought it over afterwards, it occurred to her that she ought to have wondered at this, but at the time it all seemed quite natural); but when the Rabbit actually took a watch out of its *waistcoat-pocket*, and looked at it, and then hurried on, Alice started to her feet, for it flashed across her mind that she had never before seen a rabbit with either a waistcoat-pocket, or a watch to take out of it, and, burning with curiosity, she ran across the field after it, and was just in time to see it pop down a large rabbit-hole under the hedge.

Alice in Wonderland

by
Lewis Carroll

In another moment down went Alice after it, never once considering how in the world she was to get out again.

The rabbit-hole went straight on like a tunnel for some way, and then dipped suddenly down, so suddenly that Alice had not a moment to think about stopping herself before she found herself falling down what seemed to be a very deep well.

Either the well was very deep, or she fell very slowly, for she had plenty of time as she went down to look about her, and to wonder what was going to happen next. First, she tried to look down and make out what she was coming to, but it was too dark to see anything: then she looked at the sides of the well, and noticed that they were filled with cupboards and book-shelves: here and there she saw maps and pictures hung upon pegs. She took down a jar from one of the shelves as she passed: it was labeled "ORANGE MARMALADE," but to her great disappointment it was empty: she did not like to drop the jar, for fear of killing somebody underneath, so managed to put it into one of the cupboards as she fell past it.

> **Either the well was very deep, or she fell very slowly, for she had plenty of time as she went down to look about her....**

"Well!" thought Alice to herself. "After such a fall as this, I shall think nothing of tumbling downstairs! How brave they'll all think me at home! Why, I wouldn't say anything about it, even if I fell off the top of the house!" (Which was very likely true.)

Down, down, down. Would the fall *never* come to an end? "I wonder how many miles I've fallen by this time?" she said aloud. "I must be getting somewhere near the center of the earth. Let me see: that would be four thousand miles down, I think—" (for, you see, Alice had learned several things of this sort in her lessons in the schoolroom, and though this was not a *very* good opportunity for showing off her knowledge, as there was no one to listen to her, still it was good practice to say it over) "—yes, that's about the right distance—but then I wonder what Latitude or Longitude I've go to?" (Alice had not the slightest idea what Latitude was, or Longitude either, but she thought they were nice grand words to say.)

Presently she began again. "I wonder if I shall fall right *through* the earth! How funny it'll seem to come out among the people that walk with their heads downwards! The antipathies, I think—" (she was rather glad there *was* no one listening, this time, as it didn't sound at all the right word) "—but I shall have to ask them what the name of the country is, you know. Please, Ma'am, is this New Zealand? Or Australia?" (and she tried to curtsey as she spoke— fancy *curtseying* as you're falling through the air! Do you think you could manage it?) "And

44

what an ignorant little girl she'll think me for asking! No, it'll never do to ask: perhaps I shall see it written up somewhere."

Down, down, down. There was nothing else to do, so Alice soon began talking again. "Dinah'll miss me very much tonight, I should think!" (Dinah was the cat.) "I hope they'll remember her saucer of milk at tea-time. Dinah, my dear! I wish you were down here with me! There are no mice in the air, I'm afraid, but you might catch a bat, and that's very like a mouse, you know. But do cats eat bats, I wonder?" And here Alice began to get rather sleepy, and went on saying to herself, in a dreamy sort of way, "Do cats eat bats? Do cats eat bats?" and sometimes "Do bats eat cats?" for, you see, as she couldn't answer either question, it didn't much matter which way she put it. She felt that she was dozing off, and had just begun to dream that she was walking hand in hand with Dinah, and was saying to her very earnestly, "Now, Dinah, tell me the truth: did you ever eat a bat?", when suddenly, thump! Thump! Down she came upon a heap of sticks and dry leaves, and the fall was over.

Alice had not the slightest idea what Latitude was, or Longitude either, but she thought they were nice grand words to say.

Alice

by Shel Silverstein

She drank from a bottle called DRINK ME
And up she grew so tall,
She ate from a plate called TASTE ME
And down she shrank so small.
And so she changed while other folks
Never tried nothin' at all.

The Voice

by Shel Silverstein

There is a voice inside of you
That whispers all day long,
"I feel that this is right for me,
I know that *this* is wrong."
No teacher, preacher, parent, friend
Or wise man can decide
What's right for you—just listen to
The voice that speaks inside.

The Stuff That Dreams Are Made Of

When you wake up in the morning, do you remember your dreams? Can you recall the details of the dream you had last night? Maybe you dreamt about a bus-driving seal licking a lollipop. Or maybe you danced with a goldfish. Are your dreams trying to tell you something? When you dream, you are often working through the problems, fears, and worries of your waking life. Each piece of your dream is a symbol representing a feeling, desire, thought or concern you have. The symbols have broader significance that may help explain what you are dreaming about. Only you can say whether or not an interpretation of your dream is on target. Happy dreaming!

Animal Symbolism

Dreaming about animals is generally lucky and foretells of good fortune. If the animals in your dream talk, then the luck is doubled! Listen to what they have to say.

BEAVER: Hard work will grant you everything you desire.

BULL: You will have a successful and luxurious life. A bull can also represent a strong-willed, powerful person or challenge in your life.

DEER: Usually stands for someone you know, who is gentle.

DOLPHIN/WHALE: Your spiritual and intellectual sides are opening up to you. You are gaining an awareness of your unconscious self.

FISH: Good luck is headed your way, particularly if you dream of goldfish.

PONY: You are exploring your potential in all its forms.

PUPPY: New friendships will strengthen for you.

RABBITS: It is very lucky to dream of rabbits. Something very good is coming your way.

UNICORN: You are gaining clarity about an existing circumstance.

Color Symbolism

Though not always easy to see, try to pay attention to color in your dreams.

PINK: Love; healing through love

RED: Passion or anger

BLACK: Your subconscious or a void

GRAY: Fear and confusion

WHITE: Truth, cleansing, purity, and new beginnings

GREEN: Healing, growth, and newness

BLUE: Spirituality; sometimes sadness

YELLOW: Peace, hope, and happiness

Other Common Symbols

ANGELS: Peace and joy

BABY: Good fortune and helpful friends

BUS: You are making progress toward an important goal

CANDY: You will soon meet with great success

CONCERT: Good news is headed your way

DANCING: Good times are ahead

PLANE/FLYING: Freedom; escape, travel

SCHOOL: Life lessons

TELEPHONE: Your subconscious is trying to catch your attention about something.

Imagine

by John Lennon

You may say I'm a dreamer.
But I'm not the only
one. I hope some
day you'll join
us and the world
will be as one.

50

Imagine there's no heaven.
It's easy if you try.
No hell below us,
Above us only sky.
Imagine all the people
Livin' for today, Ah.

Imagine there's no countries,
It isn't hard to do,
Nothing to kill or die for
And no religion too.
Imagine all the people
Livin' life in peace.

(Chorus)

Imagine no possessions,
I wonder if you can.
No need for greed or hunger,
A brotherhood of man.
Imagine all the people
Sharing all the world.

(Chorus)

Dear Diary

Keeping a journal can be something that you do every day, every once in a while, or for special occasions. To get started, all you need is a basic composition book or a plain paper notebook. The rest is up to you! Create themed journals or add special decorative or functional elements to your book

Circle Journal

Remember the best times with your best friends forever. Spend time together to decorate and personalize a group book to share. Then, take turns with the journal so that everyone adds an entry. You might write about your deepest secrets or let each person tell her version of a shared adventure. Or start a story and have each person add a chapter. See how many times the book goes around the circle of friends in one year. Then start a new one for the next year!

Travelogue

Chart a day-by-day adventure of the next big trip you take. It might be summer camp, a tour with the school band, or a family vacation. Collect program stubs and pictures and paste them inside your journal, or slip them in picture pockets. You can decorate your journal with magazine clippings or cut up postcards that remind you of the best (and worst!) parts of your vacation.

Dream Book

Let your imagination run wild each time you add an entry. Every day, week, or month you might write a poem, a story, something silly, or simply what you did that day. See what happens if you record your dreams. Your nighttime adventures might give you ideas for your next creative writing assignment.

Slipcover

Fabric scraps (such as denim, velvet, corduroy) or wrapping paper, marker, ruler, scissors, glue

1. Lay your book open on the material you want to use for your cover.

2. Trace around the outside of the book onto the cover material. To make book flaps, measure 2 inches past the left and right sides of the book. Cut out the cover.
3. Squeeze a thin line of glue around the outside edges of the book. Press the cover material on, leaving 2-inch flaps on the left and right side. Then, fold the flaps over the ends and glue them in place.

Place-Marker Pen

Rubber cement, pen, 24-inch-long ribbon

1. Take the cap off the pen. Brush a thin layer of rubber cement covering half the pen, starting from the writing tip.
2. Hold one end of the ribbon against the writing tip of the pen and carefully wrap the ribbon around the pen like a candy cane. Tip: Hold the ribbon at an angle and twist the pen.
3. Apply rubber cement to the top half of the pen and continue wrapping ribbon around it. When the glue dries, trim any excess ribbon off the writing tip end.
4. Open the back cover of journal. Brush a thin strip of rubber cement along the inside spine and press the free ribbon end along the spine, starting at the bottom and working toward the top of the book.
5. Keep your place in your journal by folding the ribbon marker between the last pages you wrote on. Your pen will dangle out the bottom of your book, ready for your next entry!

Picture Pockets

Construction paper, scissors, glue

You can make pockets to keep ticket stubs from movies, plays, concerts and other events.

1. Cut a piece of construction paper as wide as your journal.
2. Squeeze a thin strip of glue around the sides and bottom and press it onto a page of your journal. When the glue dries, slip your stubs in the pocket and write all about your day on the opposite page.

As long as I live
I shall always be
My Self—and no other,
Just me.

Like a tree.

Like a willow or elder,
An aspen, a thorn,
Or a cypress forlorn.

Like a flower,
For its hour
A primrose, a pink,
Or a violet—
Sunned by the sun,
And with dewdrops wet.

Always just ME.

Me
by
Walter de la Mare

"Tell about Pippi Långstrump [Pippi Longstocking]," begged Karin Lindgren—Astrid Lindgren's seven-year-old daughter first coined the name in 1941 while sick in bed with pneumonia. The author didn't ask who Pippi was; she simply started to sketch an extraordinary fairy tale befitting the character's outlandish name. Pippilotta Delicatessa Windowshade Mackrelmint Efraim's daughter Longstocking is a nine-year-old phenomenon. The fiery-haired, curiously clad, free-spirited girl charms everyone she meets. The fearless freckle-faced heroine is the exact opposite of what girls were "supposed" to be: tidy, dutiful, and quiet. Nothing is "normal" in Pippi's wild world. She lives in a rickety house called Villa Villekulla with her pet monkey, Mr. Nilsson, and a horse that resides on the porch. A suitcase containing an apparently endless supply of gold coins provides for her every need. Her more refined neighbors, Annika and Tommy, hang on Pippi's every word as she unabashedly spins tales of her escapades. Lindgren (1907-2002), who wrote more than 70 books for children during her 94 years, received many honors for her work. One of the world's most widely translated authors, her books are available in more than 50 languages.

Beside Villa Villekulla was another garden and another house. In that house lived a father and mother and two charming children, a boy and a girl. The boy's name was Tommy and the girl's Annika. They were good, well brought up, and obedient children. Tommy would never think of biting his nails, and he always did exactly what his mother told him to do. Annika never fussed when she didn't get her own way, and she always looked pretty in her little well-ironed cotton dresses; she took the greatest care not to get them dirty. Tommy and Annika played nicely with each other in their garden, but they had often wished for a playmate. While Pippi was still sailing on the ocean with her father, they often used to hang over the fence and say to each other, "Isn't it silly that nobody ever moves into that house. Somebody ought to live there—somebody with children."

On that lovely summer evening when Pippi for the first time stepped over the threshold of Villa Villekulla, Tommy and Annika were not at home. They had gone to visit their grandmother for a week; and so they had no idea that anybody had moved into the house next door. On the first day after they came home again they stood by the gate, looking out onto the street, and even then they didn't know that there actually was a playmate so near. Just as they were standing there considering what they should do and

Pippi Longstocking

by
Astrid Lindgren

wondering whether anything exciting was likely to happen or whether it was going to be one of those dull days when they couldn't think of anything to play—just then the gate of Villa Villekulla opened and a little girl stepped out. She was the most remarkable girl Tommy and Annika had ever seen. She was Miss Pippi Longstocking out for her morning promenade. This is the way she looked:

Her hair, the color of a carrot, was braided in two tight braids that stuck straight out. Her nose was the shape of a very small potato and was dotted all over with freckles. It must be admitted that the mouth under this nose was a very wide one, with strong white teeth. Her dress was rather unusual. Pippi herself had made it. She had meant it to be blue, but there wasn't quite enough blue cloth, so Pippi had sewed little red pieces on it here and there. On her long thin legs she wore a pair of long stockings, one brown and the other black, and she had on a pair of black shoes that were exactly twice as long as her feet. These shoes her father had bought for her in South America so that Pippi would have something to grow into, and she never wanted to wear any others.

But the thing that made Tommy and Annika open their eyes widest of all was the monkey sitting on the strange girl's shoulder.

But the thing that made Tommy and Annika open their eyes widest of all was the monkey sitting on the strange girl's shoulder. It was a little monkey, dressed in blue pants, yellow jacket, and a white straw hat.

Pippi walked along the street with one foot on the sidewalk and the other in the gutter. Tommy and Annika watched as long as they could see her. In a little while she came back, and now she was walking backward. That was because she didn't want to turn around to get home. When she reached Tommy's and Annika's gate she stopped.

The children looked at each other in silence. At last Tommy spoke. "Why did you walk backward?"

"Why did I walk backward?" said Pippi. "Isn't this a free country? Can't a person walk any way she wants to? For that matter, let me tell you that in Egypt everybody walks that way, and nobody thinks it's the least bit strange."

"I have been all over the world and seen many things stranger than people walking backward."

"How do you know?" asked Tommy. "You've never been in Egypt, have you?"

"I've never been in Egypt? Indeed I have. That's one thing you can be sure of. I have been all over the world and seen many things stranger than people walking backward. I wonder what you would have said if I had come along walking on my hands the way they do in Farthest India."

"Now you must be lying," said Tommy.

Pippi thought a moment. "You're right," she said sadly, "I am lying."

"It's wicked to lie," said Annika, who had at last gathered up enough courage to speak.

"Yes, it's very wicked to lie," said Pippi even more sadly. "But I forget it now and then. And how can you expect a little child whose mother is an angel and whose father is king of a cannibal island and who herself has sailed on the ocean all her life—how can you expect her to tell the truth always? And for that matter," she continued, her whole freckled face lighting up, "let me tell you that in the Congo there is not a single person who tells the truth. They lie all day long. Begin at seven in the morning and keep on until sundown. So if I should happen to lie now and then, you must try to excuse me and to remember that it is only because I stayed in the Congo a little too long. We can be friends anyway, can't we?"

"Oh, sure," said Tommy and realized suddenly that this was not going to be one of those dull days.

I would urge you to be as impudent as you dare. BE BOLD, BE BOLD, BE BOLD!
—Susan Sontag

Figure Drawing

Anyone ever tell you to "lose the attitude"? Well, in this activity you need to find some attitude! When drawing the figure of a person, it is not enough to rely on facial expression. Body language is also very important. In the following drawings, the features of the face have been entirely left out, but the emotion is just as obvious from the attitude of the figures.

Despair

Despair brings with it a feeling of helplessness and the desire to gain the comfort of friends.

Horror

A sudden horror is revolting, and a natural impulse is to push the horror away, and to try to hide the eyes.

Confidence

A confident person walks with a firm step, with head held high and shoulders back.

Boredom

A bored person does not take interest in his surroundings, and is unlikely to show any great interest in his personal appearance. You will find him slouching along with his hands in his pockets.

Exaltation

Your first inclination on receiving sudden good news is to jump with joy.

Eagerness

A person who is eager is lively and energetic, and most probably in a hurry.

Dejection

Anyone who is under a great sorrow will often show it in his limp bearing and bowed head.

Politeness

A polite person is kindly, affable and ready to help others.

Thought

A thoughtful person is usually quiet, and will often put his hand to his chin while thinking deeply.

Movement

You can express movement just as easily as you can express moods with simple drawings. Practice capturing mood and movement with a few lines. Then add the body around the lines. You will find your figure drawings becoming more lifelike.

AMELIA EARHART (1897–1937) became the first female passenger on a flight across the Atlantic Ocean in 1928, and four years later she went on to become the first woman to make that same flight alone. Then, after Earhart flew by herself from Hawaii to the American mainland, she became the first person to fly solo across the Pacific and the first person to fly both the Atlantic and Pacific Oceans alone. After this feat, Amelia decided to fly completely around the world. Two thirds of the way into her trip, she disappeared. Though her plane was never found, Amelia Earhart has never been forgotten.

ANNE FRANK (1929–45) was born in Germany, but when the anti-Jewish government of Adolf Hitler and the Nazis came to power, she and her family fled to Holland, where it was safer. When Anne was

HEROINES OF COURAGE

11, the Nazis came to Holland. When she was 13th, Anne and her family hid themselves in a sealed office above a warehouse. For twenty-five months, they all stayed inside the few small rooms, and Anne kept a diary that she filled with her courage, humor, and wisdom. Sadly, she and her family were discovered and sent to concentration camps. Only Anne's father survived, but he later found her diary and had it published. Since then, it has been translated into over sixty-five languages and has become one of the most widely read and loved books in the world.

HELEN KELLER (1880–1968) was only 18 months old when she lost her sight and hearing due to an illness. There was not much hope for a normal life. When she was 7, a woman named Annie Sullivan was hired to teach her, and just one month later, Helen was able to associate water with the letters w-a-t-e-r, which Sullivan spelled into the little girl's palm. She understood thirty more words by the end of the same day. Helen learned very quickly, and eventually became the first deaf-blind person to graduate from college. While there, she published her life story and went on to write eleven more books. Keller spent her life touring the world delivering lectures on how to help the disabled, on peace, and on women's rights.

HARRIET TUBMAN (1820–1913) was born into slavery in Maryland to parents who were from Africa. She had a very hard life and was hired out to labor in the fields when she was only 12. When she was 29, she learned she was going to be sold and shipped to the deep South, where things were even harder for slaves. Instead, she ran away. She made it through 90 miles of swamps and woods to the North on what was called the Underground Railroad. It wasn't really under-ground or a railroad, but it was a secret path to freedom. Over the following years, she secretly returned to bring back her family and others, eventually making nineteen trips to rescue over three hundred slaves.

A Bounty of Braids

Whether your hair is long or short, curly or straight, you can give your 'do a new twist with different braids. A braid is like a rope that you can tie in knots, coil into a bun, or dangle in loops. You can even braid your braids. Once you get started on your own hair you might want to open a mini salon and braid your friends' tresses, too!

Basic Braid

Make a ponytail, two pigtails, or many minis. It's all in the part.

1. Separate the hair into three even sections.
2. Cross the left strand over the middle.
3. Cross the right strand over the new middle strand so that it becomes the middle strand. Grasp the hair snugly as you go to keep the braid from loosening.
4. Continue to cross the left strand over the middle strand, then the right strand over the middle strand.
5. Tie the end with a hair band.

SOME IDEAS:

- Before you braid, gather your hair into a small covered band. Loop a ribbon through the band and make the length even on both sides. Align the ribbon with the left and right strands as you begin to braid.

- String beads onto mini braids. Tie the ends off with embroidery thread to keep the beads on.
- Knot a small section of hair with strands of embroidery thread. Bind the thread around the hair and tie another knot at the end.

French Braid

1. Pick up the top section of hair in the area you want to braid.
2. Separate into three strands and braid left over middle, then right over middle.
3. Gather some hair into the new left strand and cross it over the middle. Repeat for the right strand.

4. Continue to weave bits of hair into the left and right strands as you braid.

Cornrow

1. Part your hair down the middle. Then part each side into small equal rows.
2. Gather a small section of hair at the top of your first row and separate it into three strands.
3. Cross the left strand under the middle.
4. Cross the right strand under the middle.
5. Gather a small bit of hair from the scalp into the left strand and cross it under the middle. Repeat for the right side.
6. Continue to gather hair from your scalp into the left and right strands as you braid.
7. Tie and continue braiding the other rows.

These braids can last several days. Just wrap your hair in a scarf when you sleep to keep them neat.

Hair Weave

1. Separate your hair into five strands.
2. Weave the first strand on the left over the second one, then under the third strand, over the fourth, and under the fifth.
3. Start on the left side again and repeat.

According to
Emily Post

Emily Post is synonymous with etiquette and her book Etiquette in Society, in Business, in Politics, and at Home, *published in 1922, is the guide to good manners and proper social behavior. While one cannot be expected to live out her thousands of tips on every situation, here are a few basic ones that will impress adult company—if that is your wish!*

Table Manners

One should make it a habit to wash one's hands and face before coming to the table.

One takes small bites.

One does not float food down one's throat with drinks.

Food noises are not acceptable. Lips are not smacked, drinks are not gulped.

Napkins, not sleeves or hands, are for wiping mouths and they are meant to be used regularly throughout the meal. Why? Because it is hard for anyone to know if he has a milk moustache or ketchup on his cheek.

Dining Dos and Don'ts

Do remember to say "please" and "thank you" frequently.

Don't *ever* put liquid into your mouth if it is already filled with food.

Don't leave food on your spoon or fork to be waved about during conversation. In fact, don't ever wave your utensils in the air.

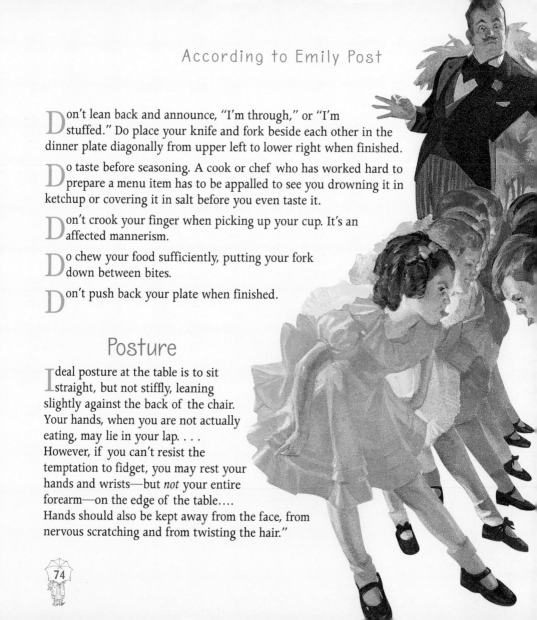

Don't lean back and announce, "I'm through," or "I'm stuffed." Do place your knife and fork beside each other in the dinner plate diagonally from upper left to lower right when finished.

Do taste before seasoning. A cook or chef who has worked hard to prepare a menu item has to be appalled to see you drowning it in ketchup or covering it in salt before you even taste it.

Don't crook your finger when picking up your cup. It's an affected mannerism.

Do chew your food sufficiently, putting your fork down between bites.

Don't push back your plate when finished.

Posture

Ideal posture at the table is to sit straight, but not stiffly, leaning slightly against the back of the chair. Your hands, when you are not actually eating, may lie in your lap. . . . However, if you can't resist the temptation to fidget, you may rest your hands and wrists—but *not* your entire forearm—on the edge of the table.... Hands should also be kept away from the face, from nervous scratching and from twisting the hair."

The Napkin

Ordinarily, as soon as you are seated you put your napkin on your lap. At a formal dinner, however, you wait for your hostess to put hers on her lap first. It does not matter how you do so, so long as you do not give it a violent shake to open it up.

No one should ever tuck a napkin into one's collar, belt, or between the buttons of one's shirt.

When using the napkin avoid wiping your mouth as if with a washcloth. Blotting or patting the lips is much more attractive.

When the meal is finished, put the napkin on the left side of your place, or if the plates have been removed, in the center.

"Please Pass the Jelly"

It is correct to reach for anything on the table that does not necessitate stretching across your neighbor or leaning far across the table yourself. When something is out of reach, simply ask the person nearest to it, "Would you please pass the jelly, Peter?"

The Silver: From the Outside In

There should never be any question of which silver to use: You always start with the implement of each type that is farthest from the plate.

When you have finished the main course the knife and fork are placed beside each other in the dinner plate diagonally from upper left to lower right. The handles extend slightly over the edge of the plate.

How to Hold Flatware

It is surprising how many people grip their eating utensils with their hands in a fist. It is much more comfortable to hold them lightly. The fork and spoon are held with the thumb and forefinger at a position on the fork that is comfortable, usually about three-quarters of the way up the handle. Your other three fingers then fit loosely and comfortably behind the handle, with the middle finger serving as a support from underneath.

Using the Knife and Fork

The American custom of 'zigzag' eating (changing the fork from left to right hand after cutting meat) is perfectly correct, but I feel that it is unnecessarily complicated. It does not have so pleasing an appearance as the simpler European method of leaving the fork in your left hand after you have cut your meat. You eat the meat from your fork while it is still in the left had, prongs down, rather than turning the fork over and switching it to your right hand.

Grooming at the Table

The one never-to-be-broken rule is Never use a comb at a restaurant table—or in any public place. Never rearrange or put your hands to your hair in any place where food is served. These rules apply to both men and women.

Other Helpful Tips from Ms. Post

Responding to Compliments

Don't simper and don't belittle whatever the compliment referred to. For instance if someone says, 'What a lovely dress,' don't say, 'Oh, well, it was very inexpensive, and I don't think it fits very well.' The appropriate way to respond to a compliment is to say 'Thank you,' or 'I'm so glad you like it.'

Tactless Blunders

If you have any sense, you won't talk to your grandmother about how you dread getting old, to a disabled person about what fun skating is, or to a city dweller about your feelings on urban crime, dirt, congestion and noise.

"How Old Are You?"

Many people do not like to be asked their age, and it is a thoughtless question.

When the Conversation Stalls

Another helpful gambit—and one that wins instant popularity— is to ask advice.

The Caller

I cannot emphasize strongly enough how helpful and courteous it is to give your name as soon as the person at the other end answers your call. What name you give depends on how well you know, or are known to, the person who answers.

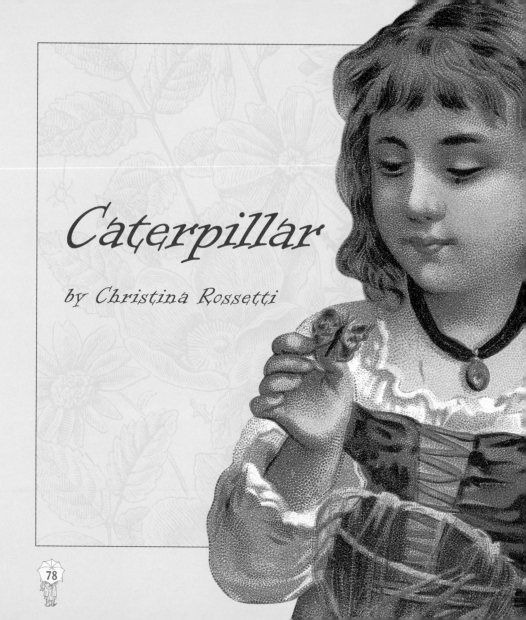

Caterpillar

by Christina Rossetti

Brown and furry
  Caterpillar in a hurry,
Take your walk
To the shady leaf, or stalk,
Or what not,
    Which may be the chosen spot.
      No toad spy you,
        Hovering bird of prey pass by you;
        Spin and die,
          To live again a butterfly.

There are so many ways to turn a plain old PB & J lunch in to a picnic. Pack several little containers of fruits and nuts for munching. You can make hummus after school and pack it in small containers for dipping veggies or pita. Turn pickles into green thumbs or apples into sticky grannies. Have some pasta salad instead of a sandwich for a change. Lunchtime never has to be the same again!

Sackable Snackables

Creamy Hummus
with Pita & Cucumber

FOR HUMMUS:
>   1 (15-ounce) can chickpeas
>   8 ounces plain yogurt
> $1/4$ cup lemon juice
> $1/4$ cup tahini paste
>   1 to 2 cloves garlic, crushed
>   1 tablespoon fresh parsley
>   2 tablespoons olive oil
>   salt to taste

In blender, combine all ingredients and whip until smooth and creamy. Store in airtight container in refrigerator.

>   Makes 2 cups (6 to 8 servings).

FOR PITA:
>   1 slice pita bread, cut into 8 triangular sections
> $1/2$ small cucumber, peeled and thinly sliced

Keep pita, cucumbers, and hummus in separate containers to prevent sogginess. At lunchtime, spread a bit of hummus on a pita triangle and top with a few cucumber slices. Yum!

Fruit Kabobs &
Dipping Sauce

FOR DIP:
>   1 cup plain yogurt
>   3 tablespoons honey
> $1/2$ teaspoon vanilla extract
> $1/2$ teaspoon almond extract

Whisk all ingredients together thoroughly and chill.

>   Makes one cup (about 4 servings).

FOR KABOBS:
>   grapes
>   blueberries
>   mandarin orange segments
>   strawberries
>   kiwi slices
>   melon cubes
>   mini-marshmallows

Spear various combinations of fruit and marsh-mallows onto toothpicks or shish kabob skewers and enjoy with dipping sauce!

Pasta Olé Salad

2 cups cooked small pasta, such as shells, wagon
    wheels, or macaroni twists
$1/2$ cup corn, cooked
$1/2$ cup black beans
$1/4$ cup black olives, sliced
$1/2$ cup grape tomatoes, halved
1 tablespoon red onion, chopped (optional)
$1/2$ small red bell pepper, chopped
$1/2$ teaspoon chili powder (optional)
$1/4$ teaspoon cumin
$1^1/2$ teaspoons fresh cilantro, chopped
2 tablespoons olive oil
$1^1/2$ teaspoons vinegar
2 teaspoons honey

1. In large bowl, toss cooked pasta with corn,
   black beans, olives, tomatoes, onion, and
   bell pepper.
2. In small dish, whisk together chili powder,
   cumin, cilantro, olive oil, vinegar, and honey.
   Pour dressing over pasta salad and toss until
   salad ingredients are well coated. Keep
   refrigerated.

Makes about 1 quart (4 to 6 servings).

Honey Bunny Salad

3 cups shredded carrots
$1/2$ cup raisins
$1/2$ cup plain yogurt
1 tablespoon honey

Toss all ingredients together until well blended.

Makes 4 to 6 servings.

Green Thumb

small flour tortilla
large pickle
1–2 tablespoons cream cheese

Spread cream cheese onto tortilla. Place pickle
on lower third of tortilla. Fold sides in, then
fold bottom third over pickle and roll closed.

Sticky Grannies

1 Granny Smith apple
2 tablespoons peanut butter
1 teaspoon shredded coconut
2 teaspoons golden raisins (optional)

Cut apple in half and core. Spread peanut butter across apple halves and sprinkle with coconut. Press raisins in center. Close apple halves together and wrap for school lunch.

Super Lunch-Sack Stuffers

- Pickles
- Chocolate-marshmallow spread sandwiched between graham crackers
- Pretzels or popcorn
- Bananas, apples or grapes
- Peeled orange
- Baby carrots
- Cherry tomatoes
- Yogurt cups
- Pudding cups
- Applesauce
- Juice boxes
- Crackers with sliced cheese and salami
- Fortune cookies
- String cheese
- Hard-boiled eggs
- Fig bars
- Edamame
- Sunflower seeds
- Peanuts in shells
- Homemade cookies or brownies

Better Brown Bag Tips:

- Put juice boxes or water bottles in freezer the night before. You'll have a cold drink for lunch and an ice pack to keep the rest of your lunch cool.
- Keep lettuce, tomatoes, and other "moist" foods wrapped separately. Build your sandwich at lunchtime and avoid soggy sammies!
- Pack travel-size moist hand wipes for easy cleanup after you eat.
- Thermoses can be for more than just juice. You can keep last night's leftover spaghetti, chili, or soup warm for several hours. Or, keep pasta salads, potato salad, or fruit salads nice and cool.
- Save prepackaged condiments from your favorite take-out restaurants for extra breadspreads or dipping sauces.

83

Distractions

by M. J. Redman

What *is* the good of asking me
for nine times four,
When a pixie keeps on nodding roun
the schoolroom door?

What *is* the good of looking
at a map of Greece,
When a baby elf is rolling
on the mantelpiece?

What *is* the good of telling me
about King John,
When the *fairy* on the
window-sill
keeps dancing on?

What *is* the good of asking me
to learn a scale,
When a *brownie* sits
and chuckles
on the picture-rail?

Harriet M. Welsch (the "M" doesn't stand for anything) is no ordinary eleven-year-old. She is independent, rude, imaginative, clever . . . and she is a bona fide spy. The child of well-meaning but neglectful parents, Harriet has a lot of free time on her hands, which she fills with a regular "spy route." She peers through windows at her "subjects" and makes scribblings about them in her trusty notebook. Harriet writes constantly—she's filled fourteen notebooks since the time she was eight. This complicated sixth grader takes herself and her WORK (she writes in all capital letters) very seriously. She is determined to become a writer one day. Things turn sour for Harriet when her classmates confiscate her secret spy notebook and read the contents aloud. Everyone in her class finds something in there about themselves—and it's not all good-natured. An ostracized Harriet struggles to learn what it means to be honest and what it means to be a friend. With the help of her kind, erudite nanny, Ole Golly, and her compassionate, forgiving pals, Harriet just might make it.

"What do you have in school this year, Harriet?" asked Ole Golly.

"English, History, Geography, French, Math, ugh, Science, ugh, and the Performing Arts, ugh, ugh, ugh." Harriet rattled these off in a very bored way.

"What history?"

"Greeks and Romans, ugh, ugh, ugh."

"They're fascinating."

"What?"

"They are. Just wait, you'll see. Talk about spies. Those gods spied on everybody all the time."

"Yeah?"

"'Yes,' Harriet, not 'yeah.'"

"Well, I wish *I'd* never heard of them."

"Ah, there's a thought from Aesop for you: 'We would often be sorry if our wishes were gratified.'" Ole Golly gave a little moo of satisfaction after she had delivered herself of this.

"I think I'll go now," Harriet said.

"Yes," said the cook, "go out and play."

Harriet stood up. "I do not go out to PLAY, I go out to WORK!" and in as dignified a way as possible she walked from the room

Harriet the Spy

by Louise Fitzhugh

87

and up the steps from the kitchen. Then she began to run, and running furiously, she went past the first floor with the living room and dining room, the second floor with her parents' bedroom and the library, and on up to the third floor to her little room and bath.

Harriet loved her room. It was small and cozy, and the bathroom was a little one with a tiny window which looked out over the park across the street. Her room had a bigger window. She looked around, pleased as always by the order, the efficiency of it. She always picked up everything immediately, not because anyone nagged at her—no one ever had—but because it was her room and she liked to have it just so. Harriet was just so about a lot of things. Her room stood around her pleasantly, waiting for her. Her own small bed next to the window, her bookcase filled with her books, her toy box, which had been filled with toys but which now held her notebooks because it could be locked, her desk and chair at which she did her homework—all seemed to look back at her with affection. Harriet put her books down on the desk and hurriedly began to change into her spy clothes.

Her spy clothes consisted first of all of an ancient pair of blue jeans, so old that her mother had forbidden her to wear them, but which Harriet loved because she had fixed up the belt with hooks to carry her spy tools. Her tools were a flashlight, in case she were ever out at night, which she never was, a leather pouch for her notebook, another leather case for extra pens, a water canteen, and a boy scout knife which had, among other features, a screwdriver and a knife and fork which collapsed. She had never had occasion to eat anywhere, but someday it might come in handy.

She attached everything to the belt, and it all worked fine except that she rattled a little. Next she put on an old dark-blue sweatshirt with a hood which she wore at the beach house in the summer so that it still smelled of salt air in a comforting way. Then she put on an old pair of blue sneakers with holes over each of their little toes. Her mother had actually gone so far as to throw these out, but Harriet had rescued them from the garbage when the cook wasn't looking.

Harriet loved her room. It was small and cozy, and the bathroom was a little one with a tiny window.

She finished by donning a pair of black-rimmed spectacles with no glass in them. She had found these once in her father's desk and now sometimes wore them even to school, because she thought they made her look smarter.

She stood back and looked at herself in the full-length mirror which hung on her bathroom door. She was very pleased. Then she ran quickly down the steps and out, banging the front door behind her.

Spy Games

*H*arriet the Spy kept a notebook to record her friends' activities. But she made one mistake: She didn't encrypt her messages! With a little invisible ink and a pocket decoder, you can be a master of espionage— and you won't have to worry if you lose your journal on your spy route. So the next time you plan to meet a friend after school, encode your message and keep your secrets safe.

Invisible Ink Notes

Lemon, small dish, toothpick, paper, electric lamp or iron

1. To make invisible ink, squeeze some juice from a lemon into a small dish.
2. Dip the end of a toothpick into the "ink" and write your message on a piece of paper. Let it dry.
3. When you are ready to reveal the message, hold the paper close to a light bulb that's turned on. For quicker results, ask an adult to go over the paper with a hot iron.

Secret Wrappers

Paper, scissors, pencil, tape

1. Cut a thin, long strip of paper.
2. Wind the paper tightly around the pencil like the stripes on a candy cane. Tape it down at both ends to hold it in place temporarily.
3. Write a message along the length of the pencil. Unwrap the paper and see how your message is instantly encrypted!
4. Pass the note to a friend and have her wind the paper up on a pencil to read your message.

Three-Way Decoder Ring

Drawing compass, construction paper, scissors, brad, marker ruler (Do this with a friend and make matching decoders!)

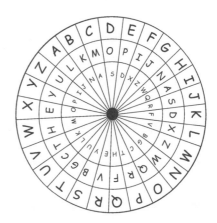

1. Use a compass to draw three circles that are 5 inches, 6 inches, and 7 inches in diameter on construction paper.
2. To construct your decoder, cut out the circles and stack them on top of one another from largest to smallest. Poke a brad through the centers of all three circles and fold the prongs open underneath.
3. On the edge of the largest circle (your outer ring), write every letter of the alphabet and, if desired, numerals 0 through 9. Make sure they're evenly spaced.
4. Use a ruler to draw a line between every letter and numeral toward the center of your decoder. The lines should extend over the middle and inner circles.
5. In between the lines on the middle ring, write your letters and, if desired, numerals. This time, instead of writing the letters and numbers in order, mix them up. You might write them backward, or in a pattern, such as A, Z, B, Y, C, X, etc.
6. Do the same thing for the inner ring, but follow a different pattern from the one you

used for the middle ring.

7. To create a code, turn the outer, middle, or inner ring and match up a new set of letters.
8. Write a secret message to a friend with a key to decode the message. For example, the key *MB-IG*, could mean line up the middle ring letter B with the inner ring letter G.

Hidden in Plain Sight

A quick way to write a secret message is to hide it in the first letter of every word of another message. See if you can find the hidden message in the following sentences: Lucy eats turkey sausage meatballs every eleventh Thursday in Nebraska. Twelve hungry elves try riding elegant elephants. Harriet once used secret encoders.*

*Let's meet in the treehouse.

The most important part of the body is the brain.

—FRIDA KAHLO

What are cells?

The cell is the basic unit of all living things. Your body is made up of billions of them! Each cell has three main parts: the nucleus (basically the cell's brain in the center of the cell; the nucleus tells each part of the cell what to do), cytoplasm (the fluid that surrounds the nucleus; where energy is produced) and the cell membrane (the outside of the cell, which allows substances to travel in and out of the cell; it also holds the cell together). Each type of cell has a different shape and performs a different task. For example, muscle cells contract and relax to create motion, while brain cells transmit signals to and from your brain. Different organisms have different cell structures. Your body's cell structure is different from your pet's; your pet's cell structure, in turn, is different from a plant's.

What are minerals?

Our body requires minerals in order to survive. Minerals are inanimate substances that help our body function. They help build bones and teeth, carry oxygen in the bloodstream, help nerves function and are an essential component of all kinds of tissue. Food supplies the minerals we need. It is a good idea to eat a varied diet, since different foods contain different minerals.

Why is blood red?

Blood is actually made up of colorless cells (called white blood cells), platelets, red cells, and other substances (including a liquid called plasma, which is mostly made of water and proteins). Blood is composed mainly of red cells (approximately 45 percent), which gives the substance its distinct color. Red cells carry oxygen around the body and get rid of waste, while white cells combat germs, and platelets help with clotting.

What are organs?

Organs are structures within your body that perform certain tasks. Your heart is an organ. When we think of a particular group of organs that have related functions, we often say they work together as a system. For example, your digestive system (which converts the foods and drinks you swallow into smaller, digestible parts) and respiratory system (which does your breathing for you) are made up of groups of organs.

How does the heart work?

Your heart, which never stops beating, is what keeps you alive. The heart is a hollow, pumplike organ whose tissue (cardiac muscle) relaxes and contracts in order to move blood through your body. The heart's job is to supply oxygen-rich blood to all the cells in your body. Your arteries (tubes) move the oxygen-rich blood away from the heart to your tissues, cells, and organs. Veins, on the other hand, are vessels that move deoxygenated blood from parts of the body (tissues, cells, and organs) back to the heart and lungs.

Your heart is about as large as your fist when you're a kid and as large as two fists when you're an adult.

What are senses? And how many do we have?

We have five senses: touch, taste, smell, sight, and hearing. We sense things through receptors that send signals to our brain. For instance, when you taste something, the receptors on your tongue (contained in small clusters called taste buds) interact with the chemicals in the food. The receptors than send this information to your brain.

There are only four areas of taste receptors on your tongue— sour, sweet, salty, and bitter.

How do we see?

Light first passes through the cornea of your eye, then the aqueous humor, lens and vitreous humor before it reaches the retina. The retina is a structure that contains two types of cells: rods (handle low-light vision) and cones (provide color vision and details in higher illuminations). When rods and cones (also known as photoreceptors) detect light, they send messages to the brain, which in turn translates the messages into images. There are over 120 million rods and over 6 million cones in each of your eyes.

Science Tricks

It is fun to explore the many mysteries of the world of science. Use these experiments to surprise your friends. They will think you are a genius or a great magician!

Friction

two shallow bowls of water, tennis ball, smooth rubber ball

1. Place the tennis ball in one bowl and the rubber ball in the other.
2. Ask your friend to tell you which ball they think will go faster when spun.
3. Spin each ball and observe how they move in water. The rubber ball will move faster.

PRINCIPLES AT WORK: Smooth surfaces cause less friction than rough ones. Friction makes it harder for the rough tennis ball to move whether it's on a solid surface or in the water.

Surface Tension

strainer, cooking oil, shallow bowl, small glass of water

1. Coat the wire mesh of your strainer with cooking oil either by pouring it through the strainer into the bowl or dipping the strainer into a small bowl of oil.
2. Holding the coated strainer over the sink, carefully add the glass of water. The water should stay inside of the strainer.
3. Ask your friend to touch the underside of the strainer with their fingers or a toothpick. The water should run out of the strainer into the sink.

Science Tricks

PRINCIPLES AT WORK: The water stays inside the strainer at first because the oil coats the rough wire and creates a "skin" of surface tension. The molecules of water already have a very strong attraction, and the oil helps reinforce the attraction to fight against gravity and the sharp edges of the wire mesh. The surface tension bonds are broken once your friend's hand or toothpick breaks the surface of the oil.

Static Electricity
nickel, flat toothpick, clear plastic cup, balloon

1. Place your nickel on its edge and balance the flat toothpick on top.
2. Cover both objects with the plastic cup.

3. Rub your balloon back and forth across your sweater, your hair, or the carpet to create a "charge."
4. Hold the charged balloon near the cup and move it around. This will cause the toothpick to move in tandem with the balloon.

PRINCIPLES AT WORK: Rubbing the balloon against your hair, sweater or the carpet causes it to become negatively charged with electrons. The negatively charged electrons are attracted to the positively charged particles of the toothpick. The attraction between the two is strong enough to cause the toothpick to move.

Do You Believe In Magic

by John Sebastian

If you believe in magic come along with me.
We'll dance until morning
'Til there's just you and me.
And maybe baby if the music is right.
I'll meet you tomorrow and we'll go late at night.
And we'll go dancin' baby
Then you'll see
How the magic's in the music
And the music's in me.

If you believe
in magic come
along with me.
We'll dance
until morning
'til there's just
you and me.

GET COLLECTING!

*S*tarting a collection takes only a thirst for hunting down items and a passion for your hobby. Sometimes it doesn't even have to cost you a penny. You can collect just about anything—from beads, bracelets, and bottle caps to seashells, stickers, and snow globes!

BEADS

*A*round the world, beads have been a popular cultural symbol for thousands of years. In many countries, beads were (and still are!) worn as decoration and as badges of wealth and royalty, used for magic and healing powers, and thought of as cherished posessions. Beads are made from just about anything—clay, glass, wood, precious rocks, cloth, and metal.

Hunting for beads can be a lot of fun! They can be found anywhere, from stores and markets to garage sales and antique shops. Once you have started your collection, the next fun step is deciding what to do with your beads! You can separate them by material, color, shape, and size in boxes, or you can use them—wear them, decorate little boxes or picture frames, string them as holiday wreaths, give them as gifts.

BEANIE BABIES

The first nine Beanie Babies hit the market in 1993, and their creator, Ty Warner, quickly figured out that the way to keep people interested was to limit supply. He sold the adorable little beanbag creatures only to small stores, keeping people guessing where to find the newest ones. Without any advertising or promotions, Beanie Babies turned into a nationwide craze, which intensified once the company began retiring Beanies regularly. There are now countless websites, publications, and clubs devoted to swapping and collecting

FACT: *The first nine Beanie Babies were Brownie the bear, Chocolate the moose, Flash the dolphin, Legs the frog, Patti the platypus, Pinchers the lobster, Splash the whale, Spot the dog, and Squealer the pig.*

the wee beanbag toys, and the hobby remains amazingly affordable—the thrill is not in collecting expensive Beanies, but in hunting them down!

When collecting Beanies, remember that the tags are very important. They have a heart tag on their ear to indicate the Ty logo and a tush tag (actually on their tush!) with the year they were made. The years distinguish different generations of Beanies. Other ways to join in the Beanie fun are to collect the Beanie Babies trading cards or pick up some Beanie Buddies, the larger version of the Beanie Babies.

DOLLS

Doll collecting is thought to be the second-biggest hobby in the U.S. (stamp collecting is the first). Of the many dolls you can collect, Cabbage Patch Kids, Madame Alexander, Barbie, and America Girl are some popular labels. There also are many different materials to choose from—dolls can be made from plastic, porcelain, cloth, wood, and paper.

When you begin your doll collection,

FACT: *In nineteenth-century America, the clothes for paper dolls did not have those tabs we see today for clipping the clothes on. Instead, children placed tiny drops of sealing wax on the dolls, which temporarily glued the clothing in place.*

you can hunt down additions in garage sales, flea markets, antique stores, craft shows, doll shops, and toy stores, depending on what kind of dolls you want to find! Many collectors take pleasure in mending and fixing dolls that are in poor condition, while enjoying the history behind well-loved dolls. Others specialize in unopened, untouched dolls in pristine condition. There are dolls for all. Just make sure you reserve plenty of space in your room to display your beautiful collection!

STAMPS

Philately, or stamp collecting, is one of the easiest hobbies to get started. After all, stamps arrive at your house every day! The hobby began in 1841 when a young girl from England wanted to decorate her walls with canceled stamps. Her advertisement in a London paper sparked a curiosity that eventually spread throughout the world. There are special editions to commemorate anniversaries and current events. They depict kings and queens, artists, writers, birds, buildings, flags, fruit, cars, historical figures—you name it. Every country has its own stamps, and the possibilities are endless. A tip on getting started from an expert philatelist: Try collecting one thing only. There are so many stamps to choose from that you need to pick a starting point. For example, collect only stamps from Finland, or only stamps with one theme (like sports or famous people).

Stamps need to be handled with clean and careful hands in order to preserve their condition for many years of enjoyment. Never peel stamps off their envelopes. If they are not the self-adhesive kind, or are not very old, soak them in warm water to loosen them, let them dry, and then put them in a book for a day to get the curl out. For the newer stamps that retain the adhesive gum after soaking, try laying them face down after soaking and then flattening them after they are completely dry. Also watch out for colorful cancellation inks—if soaked, they will run! Keep your stamps affixed to acid-free pages with stamp hinges (available at hobby stores) and store them in a binder. Never tape or glue your stamps directly onto your pages. Another way to store them is in plastic sleeves within a binder.

STICKERS

Collecting stickers is a fun and fascinating hobby, and because they come in many different shapes, sizes, styles, and colors there are endless collecting possibilities! Stickers are small, they stack and store easily, and they are easy to display and appreciate. First decide what you want to collect—you can specialize in scratch-and-sniff stickers, stickers that change color when you press on them, sparkly and shiny stickers, fuzzy and soft stickers, or even holographic stickers. You might also collect stickers of your favorite action hero, cartoon character, sport star, or even pop singer. There are websites, books, and stores dedicated to stickers, so with some research and time to wade through them, you can build an interesting collection. A little research will help you define what you are interested in and what particular stickers or series of stickers are of value.

The Topps Chewing Gum Company released Wacky Packages—peel and punch-out stickers—between 1967 and 1992. They parodied common household products and were extremely popular among children in the 1970s. These stickers have of late enjoyed a great resurgence of popularity as more and more recall this childhood craze and desire to re-collect them. If you find a 1960s or an early 1970s unopened box or pack of Wacky Packages, then hold on to it—and don't open it!! Keep your sticker collection in an album or scrapbook. This way they are portable and you can share them with friends and use your extras to decorate envelopes, letters, packages, and frames.

Scented Suds

T urn your soap dish into a bowl of lavender, roses, or orange blossoms! You can make your own spa-style scented soaps to use every day at home or give away as gifts. This project is hot! So be sure to have an adult help you with the cooking and cutting while you put your scents to the test.

Five to seven bars of pure glycerin soap, cutting board, knife, heavy pot, essential oils, glass pie plate or candy molds, ladle

1. Cut glycerin soap into small chunks and let it melt in the pot over medium heat for about 15 minutes. Do not stir.
2. Spread three drops of essential oil on the bottom of the pie plate or candy molds.
3. When the soap has melted, carefully ladle it into the plate or molds. (Be careful not to let the glycerin bubble or foam. If it does, just turn off the heat.)
4. As the soap in the glass dish starts to cool, it will harden. While it's setting, press a few herb sprigs or flower petals onto the surface (be sure you wait until it starts to cool as the soap will be super-hot)
5. Melt some more glycerin. Pour it on top of the cooled layer to seal the herbs in the middle of the soap.

6. When the soap has hardened completely, have an adult help you cut it into bars (or take it out of the molds).

FUN IDEAS:
- use cookie cutters for fun-shaped soaps
- make "chunky" soap by cutting small blocks of glycerin and adding them to the baking dish after you pour in the melted soap
- make striped soap, by melting one color, pouring it into the dish, letting it harden, then pouring a layer of differently colored soap on top.
- make your own special blends by adding some of these aromatic ingredients in steps 2 or 4: lavender, vanilla, sage, rosemary, eucalyptus, honeysuckle, rose, peppermint, gardenia, pine, almond, coconut, citrus.

Spoiled and sickly Mary Lennox spent her young childhood days being doted upon by her Ayah in India. But when a virus took her parents' lives, the orphaned girl was sent to her disagreeable uncle's Yorkshire mansion on the edge of a vast moor. So began Frances Hodgson Burnett's delightful novel. Burnett (1849-1924) wrote more than 50 books and dozens of short stories throughout her career. But it is for her three remarkable children's books—*Little Lord Fauntleroy* (1886), *A Little Princess* (1905), and particularly *The Secret Garden* (1911)—that she is best remembered. The seeds for Burnett's most famous novel were sown during her childhood in Victorian England. Growing up in the industrial city of Manchester, she dreamed of more natural surroundings. We pick up Mary's story as she begins to embrace the mysteries of life and the magical world around her. With the help of the restorative powers of nature, her gradual transformation from idle weakling to robust young woman begins to take place.

Mary skipped round all the gardens and round the orchard, resting every few minutes. At length she went to her own special walk and made up her mind to try if she could skip the whole length of it. It was a good long skip and she began slowly, but before she had gone halfway down the path she was so hot and breathless that she was obliged to stop. She did not mind much, because she had already counted up to thirty. She stopped with a little laugh of pleasure, and there, lo and behold, was the robin swaying on a long branch of ivy. He had followed her and he greeted her with a chirp. As Mary had skipped toward him she felt something heavy in her pocket strike against her at each jump, and when she saw the robin she laughed again.

"You showed me where the key was yesterday," she said. "You ought to show me the door today; but I don't believe you know!"

The robin flew from his swinging spray of ivy on to the top of the wall and he opened his beak and sang a loud, lovely trill, merely to show off. Nothing in the world is quite as adorably lovely as a robin when he shows off—and they are nearly always doing it.

Mary Lennox had heard a great deal about Magic in her Ayah's stories, and she always said that what happened almost at that moment was Magic.

One of the nice little gusts of wind rushed

The Secret Garden

by
Frances Hodgson
Burnett

down the walk, and it was a stronger one than the rest. It was strong enough to wave the branches of the trees, and it was more than strong enough to sway the trailing sprays of untrimmed ivy hanging from the wall. Mary had stepped close to the robin, and suddenly the gust of wind swung aside some loose ivy trails, and more suddenly still she jumped toward it and caught it in her hand. This she did because she had seen something under it—a round knob which had been covered by the leaves handing over it. It was the knob of a door.

She put her hands under the leaves and began to pull and push them aside. Thick as the ivy hung, it nearly all was a loose and swinging curtain, though some had crept over wood and iron. Mary's heart began to thump and her hands to shake a little in her delight and excitement. The robin kept singing and twittering away and tilting his head on one side, as if he were as excited as she was. What was this under her hands which was square and made of iron and which her fingers found a hole in?

It was the lock of the door which had been closed ten years and she put her hand in her pocket, drew out the key and found it fitted the keyhole. She put the key in and turned it. It took two hands to do it, but it did turn.

And then she took a long breath and looked behind her up the long walk to see if any-one was coming. No one was coming. No one ever

And then she took a long breath and looked behind her up the long walk to see if anyone was coming.

did come, it seemed, and she took another long breath, because she could not help it, and she held back the swinging curtain of ivy and pushed back the door which opened slowly—slowly.

Then she slipped through it, and shut it behind her, and stood with her back against it, looking about her and breathing quite fast with excitement, and wonder, and delight.

She was standing inside the secret garden.

It was the sweetest, most mysterious-looking place any one could imagine. The high walls which shut it in were covered with the leafless stems of climbing roses which were so thick that they were matted together. Mary Lennox knew they were roses because she had seen a great many roses in India. All the ground was covered with grass of a wintry brown and out of it grew clumps of bushes which were surely rosebushes if they were alive. There were numbers of standard roses which had so spread their branches that they were like little trees. There were other trees in the garden, and one of the things which made the place look strangest and loveliest was that climbing roses had run all over them and swung down long tendrils which made light swaying curtains, and here and there they had caught at each other or at a far-reaching branch and had crept from one tree to another and made lovely bridges of themselves. There were neither leaves nor roses on them now and Mary did not know whether they were dead or alive, but their thin gray or brown branches and sprays looked like a sort of hazy mantle spreading over everything, walls, and trees, and even brown grass, where they had fallen from their fastenings and run along the ground. It was this hazy tangle from tree to tree which made it all look so mysterious. Mary had thought it must be different from other gardens which had not been left all by themselves so long; and indeed it was different from any other place she had ever seen in her life.

"How still it is!" she whispered. "How still!"

Then she waited a moment and listened at the stillness. The robin, who had flown to his treetop, was still as all the rest. He did not even flutter his wings; he sat without stirring, and looked at Mary.

"No wonder it is still," she whispered again. "I am the first person who has spoken in here for ten years."

She moved away from the door, stepping as softly as if she were afraid of awakening someone. She was glad that there was grass under her feet and that her steps made no sounds. She walked under one of the fairy-like gray arches between the trees and looked up at the sprays and tendrils which formed them.

"No wonder it is still," she whispered again. "I am the first person who has spoken in here for ten years."

"I wonder if they are all quite dead," she said. "Is it all a quite dead garden? I wish it wasn't."

If she had been Ben Weatherstaff she could have told whether the wood was live by looking at it, but she could only see that there were only gray or brown sprays and branches and none showed any signs of even a tiny leaf bud anywhere.

But she was *inside* the wonderful garden and she could come through the door under the ivy any time and she felt as if she had found a world all her own.

The sun was shining inside the four walls and the high arch of blue sky over this particular piece of Misselthwaite seemed even more brilliant and soft than it was over the moor. The robin flew down from his treetop and hopped about or flew after her from one bush to another. He chirped a good deal and had a very busy air, as if he were showing her things. Everything was strange and silent and she seemed to be hundreds of miles away from anyone, but somehow she did not feel lonely at all. All that troubled her was her wish that she knew whether all the roses were dead, or if perhaps some of them had lived and might put out leaves and buds as the weather got warmer. She did not want it to be a quite dead garden. If it were a quite alive garden, how wonderful it would be, and what thousands of roses would grow on every side!

> Everything was strange and silent and she seemed to be hundreds of miles away from anyone, but somehow she did not feel lonely at all.

Her skipping-rope had hung over her arm when she came in and after she had walked about for a while she thought she would skip round the whole garden, stopping when she wanted to look at things. There seemed to have been grass paths here and there, and in one or two corners there were alcoves of evergreen with stone seats or tall moss-covered flower urns in them.

114

As she came near the second of these alcoves she stopped skipping. There had once been a flower bed in it, and she thought she saw something sticking out of the black earth—some sharp little pale green points. She remembered what Ben Weatherstaff had said and she knelt down to look at them.

"Yes, they are tiny growing things and they *might* be crocuses or snowdrops or daffodils," she whispered.

She bent very close to them and sniffed the fresh scent of the damp earth. She liked it very much.

> She bent very close to them and sniffed the fresh scent of the damp earth. She liked it very much.

"Perhaps there are some other ones coming up in other places," she said. "I will go all over the garden and look."

She did not skip, but walked. She went slowly and kept her eyes on the ground. She looked in the old border beds and among the grass, and after she had gone round, trying to miss nothing, she had found ever so many more sharp, pale green points, and she had become quite excited again.

"It isn't a quite dead garden," she cried out softly to herself. "Even if the roses are dead, there are other things alive."

She did not know anything about gardening, but the grass seemed so thick in some of the places where the green points were pushing their way through that she thought they did not seem to have room enough to grow. She searched about

until she found a rather sharp piece
of wood and knelt down and dug and
weeded out the weeds and grass
until she made nice little clear places
around them.

"Now they look as if they could breathe,"
she said, after she had finished with the first
ones. "I am going to do ever so many more. I'll do
all I can see. If I haven't time today I can come
tomorrow."

She went from place to place, and dug and weeded, and enjoyed herself so immensely that she was led on
from bed to bed and into the grass under the trees. The
exercise made her so warm that she first threw her coat
off, and then her hat, and without knowing it she was
smiling down on to the grass and the pale green points all
the time.

The robin was tremendously busy. He was very much
pleased to see gardening begun on his own estate. He had
often wondered at Ben Weatherstaff. Where gardening is
done all sorts of delightful things to eat are turned up with
the soil. Now here was this new kind of creature who
was not half Ben's size and yet had had the sense to
come into his garden and begin at once.

Mistress Mary worked in her garden until it was time to go to her midday dinner. In fact, she was rather late in remembering, and when she put on her coat and hat, and picked up her skipping-rope, she could not believe that she had been working two or three hours. She had been actually happy all the time; and dozens and dozens of the tiny, pale green points were to be seen in cleared places, looking twice as cheerful as they had looked before when the grass and weeds had been smothering them.

> Where gardening is done all sorts of delightful things to eat are turned up with the soil.

"I shall come back this afternoon," she said, looking all round at her new kingdom, and speaking to the trees and the rosebushes as if they heard her.

Then she ran lightly across the grass, pushed open the slow old door and slipped through it under the ivy. She had such red cheeks and such bright eyes and ate such a dinner that Martha was delighted.

How Does Your Garden Grow?

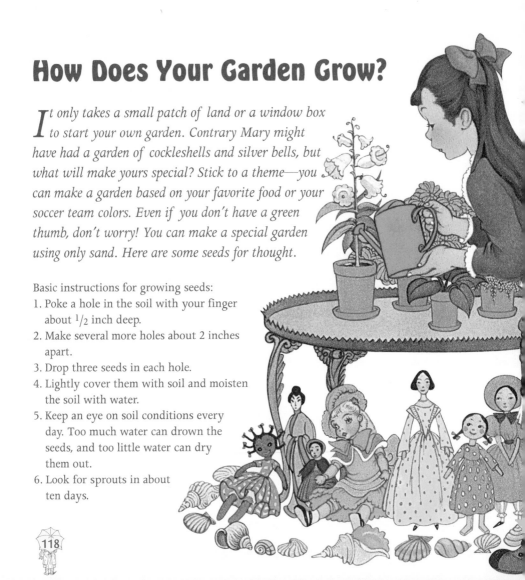

It only takes a small patch of land or a window box to start your own garden. Contrary Mary might have had a garden of cockleshells and silver bells, but what will make yours special? Stick to a theme—you can make a garden based on your favorite food or your soccer team colors. Even if you don't have a green thumb, don't worry! You can make a special garden using only sand. Here are some seeds for thought.

Basic instructions for growing seeds:

1. Poke a hole in the soil with your finger about $1/2$ inch deep.
2. Make several more holes about 2 inches apart.
3. Drop three seeds in each hole.
4. Lightly cover them with soil and moisten the soil with water.
5. Keep an eye on soil conditions every day. Too much water can drown the seeds, and too little water can dry them out.
6. Look for sprouts in about ten days.

Herb Gardens

A sure-fire way to get to eat your favorite foods more often is to plant them! Herbs are generally easy to grow from seed and like plenty of sunshine. Save some for winter by clipping them and hanging them to dry.

- Taco garden: oregano, cilantro, chives, garlic, peppers
  - Lasagna garden: basil, rosemary, thyme, oregano
    - Spaghetti garden: summer savory, oregano, marjoram, thyme
      - Gourmet garden: fennel, parsley, dill, lavender, anise

Rainbow Garden

P ut a pot of gold in your yard by planting a rainbow—but don't be surprised if you end up with more ladybugs than leprechauns. You can show off your flair for design by planting colored seeds in fun patterns. Then, come spring, watch your art bloom !

PINK: China pink, sweet William, begonia
RED: geranium, nasturtium, cockscomb
ORANGE: marigold, coneflower, California poppy
YELLOW: sunflower, zinnia, golden fleece
GREEN: alternanthera, bells-of-Ireland, ornamental kale
BLUE: forget-me-not, ageratum, blue daisy
PURPLE: cupflower, heliotrope, violet
WHITE: flowering tobacco, honesty, periwinkle

Zen Garden

D iscover the ancient secrets of Zen gardening. Imagine that the sand represents water, and the rocks, mountains. Then, smooth out the sand to clear your thoughts. Make decorative patterns to inspire creativity.

Large flat container such as a tray or box lid, sand, mini wooden rake or fork, decorative stones or shells

1. Pour the sand into your container. Make sure you have a good 2-inch layer of sand.
2. Use the small rake or fork to even out the sand and make patterns. Then arrange rocks or shells as you like. An odd number of rocks is considered lucky.
3. Whenever your mood changes, rearrange your Zen garden.

Daffodils

by

William
Wordsworth

I wandered lonely as a cloud
  That floats on high o'er vales and hills,
When all at once I saw a crowd,—
  A host of golden daffodils
Beside the lake, beneath the trees,
  Fluttering and dancing in the breeze.

Continuous as the stars that shine
  And twinkle on the Milky Way,
They stretched in never-ending line
  Along the margin of a bay:
Ten thousand saw I, at a glance,
  Tossing their heads in sprightly dance.

The waves beside them danced, but they
  Outdid the sparkling waves in glee;
A poet could not but be gay
  In such a jocund company;
I gazed—and gazed—but little thought
  What wealth the show to me had brought.

For oft, when on my couch I lie,
  In vacant or in pensive mood,
They flash upon that inward eye
  Which is the bliss of solitude;
And then my heart with pleasure fills,
  And dances with the daffodils.

SUSAN B. ANTHONY (1820–1906) came from a hardworking family in New England that gave her a strong sense of justice and morality. She grew up to be a teacher, but was fired after ten years when she complained that male colleagues made five times as much money. Anthony then became involved with anti-alcohol and anti-slavery groups, and started fighting for the rights of women. Back then, females couldn't own property, enter into contracts, or even vote. Despite opposition and abuse, Anthony traveled around the country lecturing for these basic rights. In 1860, New York State finally allowed women to own property and enter contracts. Anthony died in 1906, fourteen years before women finally won—largely due to her work—the right to vote.

ROSA PARKS (b. 1913) has been called the "mother of the Civil Rights movement." Before she changed the course of history, though, she grew up in Alabama and attended a private school for girls founded by liberal Northern women that aimed to build the self-confidence of its students. It worked. On December 1, 1955, Ms. Parks refused to give up her seat on a Montgomery bus to a white passenger and was arrested. This incident sparked a yearlong movement of blacks to boycott riding the busses. Her act of courage, heard about around the world, led the U.S. Supreme Court to declare that black people could sit anywhere they wanted.

ELEANOR ROOSEVELT (1884–1962) was more than a wife to a great U.S. president. She was a heroine in her own right. Before her White House days, she was a leader of women's organizations and helped people of all colors. Unlike previous First Ladies, Roosevelt traveled often to give lectures, had her own radio show, and wrote her own popular newspaper column. Later, after the White House years, President Truman honored her with an appointment to represent America at the United Nations. Perhaps her greatest gift was her involvement

HEROINES OF HUMAN RIGHTS

in creating the Universal Declaration of Human Rights. For the first time, a group of world leaders agreed that people around the globe should have basic rights.

GLORIA STEINEM (b. 1934) grew up taking care of her mother, who was often ill. It wasn't easy, and she escaped through reading. Her favorite book was *Little Women*, with its tales of a mom and her daughters getting by while the men were off at war. Steinem's love of words led her to become a journalist, but for a long time, her employers wouldn't let her write articles about serious subjects because she was a woman. So, in 1972, she started *Ms.*, a magazine for women, by women. It was a major success. Throughout her life, Steinem has been involved in numerous women's rights and political groups, and has inspired a generation to fight for equal rights.

Adventures A-Go-Go

On your next vacation, plan to start having fun before you pull out of the driveway. Pack an Adventure Box with scrap paper, markers, and an egg timer. You can challenge your family to a Water Tower Tournament or play rounds of Backseat Bingo. Here's a host of games that won't take up extra room in your suitcase. Bon Voyage!

Water Tower

You can keep this game going for the entire duration of the trip—even while you play other games. Every time you see a water tower, whether it's in a field or on top of a building, call it out. At the end of the trip, whoever has spotted the most water towers is the champion.

Backseat Bingo

Paper, pencil, radio

Each player makes a chart with five rows and five columns (twenty-five squares all together). In each square, write a different word that is commonly heard on the radio. (Examples include *weather, news, sports, song, hit, traffic, stocks, music, today, love.*) Players swap charts and then listen for their words on the radio. The first person to cross off a complete row, column, or diagonal wins the round.

Alphabet Spy

Each player must find three things that start with each letter of the alphabet. The first player to finish the Z's wins. For example, a Southwestern trip might include armadillos, adobes, and Appaloosas. A trip to the city might include buildings, billboards, and bridges.

Celebrity

Paper, pencil, hat or bag, timer

Each player writes the names of ten famous persons on separate scraps of paper. The names can be historical figures, current celebrities, or fictional characters. All the names get placed in the hat. One player draws names from the hat and gives clues to another player without saying any part of the name. The guessing player tries to get as many names as possible in a set amount of time. If necessary, give "sounds like" clues or break it up by syllables. For example,

Harry Potter could be "famous boy wizard" or "sounds like Cousin It from the Addams family" + "someone who makes clay bowls." The person who guesses the most names wins.

Map Hunt

Atlas or road maps, timer

One player picks out a city or landmark on a map. The other players take turns looking at the map, trying to guess the location while being timed. Each player gets 1 minute per guess. The player who guesses the location first gets a point and then picks the next spot for the others to hunt. The first person with 10 points wins and is crowned the Map Quest King or Queen.

Smoke

One player thinks of a famous person or character. The other players must guess by asking metaphorical questions. Sample questions and answers for Sherlock Holmes would be:

"If this person were a story, what kind would he or she be?" (A mystery)

"If this person were glass, what kind would he or she be?" (A magnifier)

GET SPORTY!

Tees, baskets, field goals, and nets! How many ways can you win a set? Brush up on your knowledge of some of our favorite pastimes.

TENNIS

Tennis was first played in France as early as the twelfth century, when players knocked a ball around a walled-in court with the palms of their hands. The game gradually developed the use of paddles and then racquets to hit a ball over a net. These days it's played with high-tech racquets on one of three surfaces: clay, grass, or cement. Unlike team sports, tennis has no "season," but goes year round, all over the world. There are countless tournaments and events for players to establish their rankings, but as for Grand Slams, there are only four: The Australian Open in Melbourne

(January), the French Open, near Paris (May), Wimbledon, in London, England (July), and the U.S. Open in New York City (September). The game itself has a very unusual scoring system: players score points to win games; to win a set, a player must win at least six games and lead his or her opponent by two games. The player who wins the most sets (usually two out of three) wins the match!

BASEBALL

Nobody can really be sure when baseball began in America, but some say the game started in Cooperstown, New York (home of the National Baseball Hall of Fame and Museum), in 1839. It was first played professionally in 1869, and since then the sport has grown to thirty teams in two leagues (the American and National Leagues). The regular baseball season stretches from April through September, with the two best teams (one from each league) making it to the World Series in October. The World Series is a best-of-seven showdown, alternating between the two teams' hometowns, that determines who takes home the title of champion.

BASKETBALL

Basketball was invented in 1891 by a Massachusetts gym teacher, Dr. James Naismith. Basketball moves almost without stopping and it is made up of four periods, each 12 minutes long. The twenty-nine teams in the National Basketball Association (NBA) play from October to June, with the best teams from the Eastern and Western Conferences going head to head in a best-of-seven playoff at the end.

Women's basketball has come a long way since Senda Berenson (Mrs. Abbott) adapted Naismith's rules in 1893. The Women's National Basketball Association (WNBA) came to life on June 21, 1997, when WNBA president Val Ackerman threw up the first tip for the L.A. Spark's Lisa Leslie and the New York Liberty's Kym Hampton. Since that successful inaugural season, the WNBA has expanded from eight to sixteen teams, and its games regularly draw more than 10,000 fans to the arenas.

FACT: *The Detroit Pistons scored the most points in the NBA in a single game. On December 13, 1983, Detroit beat the Denver Nuggets 186 to184 in triple overtime.*

FOOTBALL

American football's origins can be found in the rough British sport of rugby, which was brought over to the United States in the mid-1800s. The boys at Harvard College changed some rules (including the use of a new egg-shaped ball) and called it "football," but it wasn't until 1880 that a student at Yale came up with the rules for modern football. The rules have continued to change over the years, as have the setup of leagues, conferences, and so forth. Currently there is only one league—the National Football League (NFL)—divided into the American and National Football Conferences. The cream of these crops play each other in the hyped-up extravaganza known as the Super Bowl—one game, held in January. The regular season lasts from September to early January, with the thirty-two teams playing just one game per week. If you've ever watched a football game and seen how brutal it can be, you can understand why!

GOLF

Golf began in fourteenth-century (1300s) Scotland, where the rolling green hills, grazed clean by sheep, were ideal for knocking a little ball around. This very landscape is the model for modern golf courses around the world, set in deserts, along coasts, and among forests. Because it's spread out all over the planet, golf is in swing year round, with the best players coming out to compete on courses that are both challenging and beautiful.

SOCCER

Before the codification of official Football Association laws (which made no mention of the allowable number of players or the duration of play), soccer games were disorganized conflicts with fields as large as towns, and as many as 500 participants involved in a brutal daylong conflict. During the late nineteenth century, however, Britain began taking the game to various parts of the world, along with the two other English favorites, cricket and rugby. Of the three, soccer has become the most popular international sport. By the second Olympic Games, which were held in Paris in 1900, soccer had already been introduced as a demonstration game. Eight years later, England defeated Denmark in the first official Olympic soccer final during the 1908 London Games. The world governing body for soccer, Fédération Internationale de Football Association (FIFA), held its first meeting in 1904 in Paris. It was attended by seven member nations. Today, the fact that FIFA's international membership has swelled to over 150 national associations—rivaled only by the International Olympic Committee—gives testament to soccer's enduring legacy.

VOLLEYBALL

Most volleyball enthusiasts will place the birthplace of beach volleyball in Santa Monica, California, some time in the early 1920s. Families played in teams of six on courts set up on the beach. The first two-man beach volleyball game was also played in Santa Monica in 1930, and in 1947, the first official two-man beach tournament was held at State Beach, California. In fact, the sport can trace most of its major developments in the Golden State, but its Santa Monica heritage didn't keep it from attaining international scope. At the 1996 Atlanta Olympic Games, with twenty-four men's teams and sixteen women's teams representing their countries, beach volleyball became an official tournament event.

ICE HOCKEY

Ice hockey began about 200 years ago when schoolboys in Windsor, Nova Scotia, Canada, took the Irish game of hurling, changed the rules around, and played it on the ice of a favorite local skating pond. Since 1904, when a league was formed in the United States, ice hockey has been a professional sport, with thirty teams competing across the States and Canada. The regular season starts up in October and lasts all winter long. It winds down in April, but playoffs among the best teams extend through May. The Stanley Cup Playoffs, ice hockey's final series, are held in June.

129

Jumpin' Rope

Little Sally Water

Little Sally Water
Sitting in a saucer;
Rise, Sally, rise,
Wipe off your eyes.
Put your hand on your hip;
Don't let your backbone slip.
Turn to the East, Sally,
Turn to the West,
Turn to the one, Sally,
That you love the best.

(follow directions while jumping)

Cinderella

Cinderella, dressed in Yella'
Went upstairs to kiss a fella.'
Made a mistake and kissed a snal
How many doctors did it take?
1, 2, 3, 4, 5 . . .

(count until someone messes up)

Coffee & Tea

I like coffee, I like tea,
I like *(name of the chosen person)*
to come in with me.

(The two jump together and the second person says the rhyme. When the rhyme is done, the first person runs out, and the new chosen jumper comes in to say the rhyme)

Teddy Bear

Teddy bear, teddy bear,
  turn around.
Teddy bear, teddy bear,
  touch the ground.
Teddy bear, teddy bear,
  tie your shoes.
Teddy bear, teddy bear,
  read the news.
Teddy bear, teddy bear,
  go upstairs.
Teddy bear, teddy bear,
  say your prayers.
Teddy bear, teddy bear,
  turn out the light.
Teddy bear, teddy bear,
  say good night.
G-o-o-d-n-i-g-h-t.

(follow directions while jumping)

KNOCK, KNOCK!

Knock, knock.
> Who's there?

Sadie.
> Sadie who?

Sadie magic words
and I'll tell you.

Knock, knock.
> Who's there?

Anita.
> Anita Who?

Anita go to the
bathroom! Open up!

Knock, knock.
Who's there?
Ammonia.
Ammonia who?
Ammonia gonna to
tell you this once.

Knock, knock.
Who's there?
Amy.
Amy who?
Amy fraid
I've forgotten
my name again.

Knock, knock.
Who's there?
Nobel.
Nobel who?
No bell so I knocked!

WHO'S THERE?

Laugh as much as
possible, always laugh.
—Maya Angelou

HAVE YOU HEARD?

Have you heard the story
about the broken pencil?
Well, it's not worth telling—
there isn't any point.

Have you heard about the
artist who had no talent?
She was so bad she couldn't
even draw her blinds.

Have you heard about
the man who kept hundreds
of clocks in his house?
Someone told him
time was precious.

WHAD'YA CALL?

Whad'ya call a girl
who wants to be a
lawyer?   *Sue.*

Whad'ya call a girl
with one leg shorter
than the other?
          Eileen.

Whad'ya call a girl
who's been at the
beach all day?
          Sandy.

Whad'ya call a
girl with a sheep
on her head?
          Baa-Baa-Ra!

Waiter, there's a fly
in my soup!
*What do you want for two
dollars? An elephant?*

Waiter, there's a fly
in my soup!
*Shhhhhh. Everyone
will want one.*

Waiter, there's a fly
in my soup!
*Don't worry, it's not hot
enough to burn him.*

Waiter, there's a fly
in my soup!
*If you wanted one
with your dessert, you
should have said so!*

Waiter, there's a fly
in my soup!
*Couldn't be the cook,
he only uses them in
the raisin bread.*

WAITER, THERE'S A FLY IN MY SOUP

Tea Party for Six

Invite a group of girlfriends over for your own version of High Tea. This menu includes traditional tea sandwiches as well as classic deviled eggs. Shortbread and scones are an ideal accompaniment to tea and a perfect dessert for "ladies who lunch." Half the fun is arranging the food and making the table setting look special. Take the time to arrange things nicely. Serve tea on a tea tray with a plate of lemon wedges, a decanter of cream, and a bowl of sugar cubes.

Cucumber Tea Sandwiches

1 tablespoon cream cheese
4 slices white bread with crusts removed
1/2 cucumber, peeled and thinly sliced

Spread even amounts of cream cheese on four slices of bread. Arrange cucumber slices on two slices of bread and top with remaining slices of bread.

Herbed Tomato Sandwiches

1 tablespoon butter, softened to room temperature
1 teaspoon herbs, such as dill, basil, parsley or
    herbs de Provence
4 slices whole-wheat bread with crusts removed
2–4 tomato slices

Use a fork or mini-whisk to blend butter with herbs. Spread even amounts on four slices of bread. Arrange tomato slices on two slices of bread and top with remaining slices.

Ham & Melon Finger Sandwiches

4 slices pumpernickel bread with crusts removed
1 tablespoon butter
4 slices prosciutto or thinly sliced ham
1/8 honeydew melon, sliced into thin wedges

Butter four slices of bread and arrange ham evenly on two slices. Top with melon wedges and close sandwiches.

Cut all sandwiches diagonally, in both directions, to make four triangles per sandwich. Arrange wedges decoratively on a serving platter. Garnish with parsley sprigs.

Deviled Eggs

6 hard-boiled eggs
4 tablespoons mayonnaise
1¹/2 teaspoons Dijon mustard
1 tablespoon fresh parsley, minced
dash paprika

1. Remove eggshells and slice eggs in half lengthwise.
2. Scoop out the yolks and mash them in a bowl with mayonnaise, mustard, and parsley. With a mini-whisk or fork, beat mixture until it is light and fluffy.
3. Arrange egg whites on a plate. Spoon equal amounts of the egg-yolk mixture into the hollows of the egg whites. Sprinkle the top of each egg with a dash of paprika.

Shortbread with Strawberry Jam

2 sticks (1 cup) butter, softened to
    room temperature
¹/2 cup confectioners' sugar
2 cups flour, sifted
¹/4 teaspoon salt
strawberry jam

1. Preheat oven to 325°F.
2. In a medium-size bowl, cream the butter with a hand mixer. Gradually beat in the sugar.
3. Blend the flour and salt into the butter mixture by hand until thoroughly mixed.
4. Press the dough into an ungreased glass 9- by 9-inch pan. Pierce the dough with a fork every ¹/2 inch.
5. Bake until firm when lightly pressed in the center, about 25 to 30 minutes. (Shortbread should not be brown). Cut into squares. Arrange on serving dish with a jar of strawberry jam.

Raisin Scones

1 1/2 cups white flour
1/2 cup whole-wheat flour
1/3 cup granulated sugar
1 tablespoon baking powder
6 tablespoons chilled, unsalted butter
1/3 cup baking raisins
1/2 cups heavy whipping cream
2 large eggs, beaten

1. Preheat oven to 375°F.
2. In a large bowl, combine all-purpose and wheat flour, sugar, and baking powder.
3. Using a pastry blender or two knives, scissor fashion, cut in the butter until the mixture resembles course crumbs. Stir in the raisins, mixing well.
4. Combine heavy cream, reserving 1 table-spoon, and 1 beaten egg in a small bowl. Add to flour mixture. Stir until just moistened. Do not overmix.
5. Transfer the dough to a lightly floured surface and knead gently. Roll or pat the dough into a circle about 7 inches round and 1 1/2 inches thick.
6. Lightly flour the rim of a glass and press into dough, making perfect rounds. Repeat until all dough is used. Place the scones on an ungreased cookie sheet.
7. Whisk egg and 1 tablespoon heavy cream. Brush egg mixture over scones.
8. Bake for approximately 15 to 20 minutes, or until lightly browned.
9. These are especially delicious when served warm with butter and preserves.

A Perfect Pot of Tea

4 teaspoons tea leaves
4–5 cups water

Put tea leaves in a large (36-ounce) teapot. In a kettle, bring water just to a rolling boil and remove from heat. Pour water into teapot and allow tea leaves to steep for exactly 4 minutes. Immediately pour tea through a strainer* into six teacups.

* Or omit strainer and allow tea leaves to settle into each cup. Then have a tea-leaf reading (see page 218)!

Woven Wonders

Making hand-woven blankets and rugs is an age-old tradition of the Navajo, who claim the art was taught to them from Spider Woman. According to the myth, the first weaving tools were made out of sunshine and lightning; the first loom was made out of sky and earth. The stick loom described here has been used by the Mayans in Guatemala for centuries and is one of the earliest known looms recorded in history. With the help of a grown-up, you can have this ancient art tool at your fingertips. Then see what kinds of masterpieces you can thread together!

Stick Loom

Drill, twelve Popsicle sticks, glue

1. Ask an adult to drill a hole in the middle of eight Popsicle sticks.
2. To make the base for your loom, arrange two Popsicle sticks horizontally. The space between them should be the length of a Popsicle stick.
3. Place the eight drilled sticks in a vertical row across the two base sticks. Space them apart evenly. The tops and bottoms of the row sticks should be flush with the outer edges of the base sticks.
4. Glue the tips of the eight vertical sticks on to the two base sticks. Glue two more base sticks on the top of the vertical sticks, sandwiching the vertical sticks between the base sticks. Stack books on top of the loom for a few hours until the glue has thoroughly dried.

Setting up the Loom

*Stick loom, various colors of yarn,
belt (to wear while you weave), an
open space to weave*

1. Cut fifteen strands of yarn approximately 5-8 feet in length.
2. Feed a strand of yarn through each of the eight center holes of your loom. Tie the ends together in a knot.
3. Feed a strand of yarn through each of the seven slots of your loom. Line the ends up with the first knot and tie all fifteen strands into one knot.
4. Tie the knotted end to a solid fixture, such as table leg or a doorknob. Straighten out the strands of yarn on the other end and pull them taut through the loom. Tie the loose ends together in a knot and attach them to your belt.
5. Sit or stand so that the yarn is taut through the loom. Now when you lift the loom, the strands through the holes will be raised and the strands through the slots will slide to the bottom. When you lower the loom, the strands through the holes will be pulled down, while the ones in the slots will be at the top.

Loom Weaving

Small ball of yarn

1. To weave, pull the loom up. Pass your right hand between the top and bottom strands of yarn to keep them separated.
2. From left to right, pull a ball of yarn through the opening, unraveling as you go. Leave a few inches of slack on the left side.
3. Lower the loom. Pass your left hand between the top and bottom strands and pull the ball of yarn back through to the left side. Keep the threaded yarn snug as you weave.
4. Continue passing the ball of yarn back and forth, lifting or lowering the loom between rows.
5. When you have neared the end of your yarn, untie the knotted end from the fixture and remove the loom. Tie the loose ends in a knot and trim the ends. Do the same for the end attached to you. Now you've got what it takes to make belts, headbands, bracelets, chokers, bookmarks . . . you name it!

143

Little orphaned Heidi—short for Adelheid—lives with her mother's sister in the Swiss village of Mayenfeld. But when Aunt Detie gets a new job in Frankfurt, she brings her niece up the mountain to live with her grandfather. Heidi's grandfather has a reputation for being evil and mean. Ever since he stopped going to church and keeps to himself on the mountaintop, the townspeople call him Uncle Alp. But Heidi and her grandfather soon fit together like a hand in a glove. She loves her new mountain home, and doesn't wish to be anywhere else. Johanna Spyri (1827-1901) grew up in the village of Hirzel, Switzerland. She was a prolific writer during her lifetime, publishing nearly 50 books. *Heidi* (1880), originally called *Heidi's Years of Wandering and Learning*, secured for its author a place as one of the most beloved children's writers of all time.

Heidi was awakened next morning by a shrill whistle and as she opened her eyes a beam of sunlight came through the hole in the wall, making the hay shine like gold. At first she could not think where she was, then she heard her grandfather's deep voice outside and remembered joyfully that she had come to live in the mountains. . . . Now she jumped out of bed, full of excitement at all the new experiences awaiting her. She dressed herself as quickly as possible, then climbed down the ladder and hurried outside. Peter was waiting there with his herd and her grandfather was just bringing Daisy and Dusky from their stall. She went to say good morning to them all.

"Do you want to go up to the pasture with Peter?" asked the old man. This idea clearly delighted her. "You must have a wash first, or the sun will laugh to see you look so black."

He pointed to a tub full of water, standing in the sun beside the door, and Heidi went over to it at once and began to splash about. Uncle Alp went indoors, calling to Peter, "Come here, General of the goats, and bring your knapsack with you." Peter held out the little bag which contained his meager lunch, and watched with big eyes as the old man put in a piece of bread and a piece of cheese, both twice as big as his own.

"Take this mug too, and fill it for her twice at dinner time. She doesn't know how to drink straight from the goat as you do. She'll stay with you all day, and mind you look after her and see she doesn't fall down the ravine."

Heidi

by
Johanna Spyri

145

Heidi came running in. "The sun can't laugh at me now," she said. Her grandfather smilingly agreed. In her desire to please the sun, she had rubbed her face with the hard towel until she looked like a boiled lobster.

> "When you come home tonight, you'll have to go right inside the tub like a fish, for you'll get black feet running about with the goats."

"When you come home tonight, you'll have to go right inside the tub like a fish, for you'll get black feet running about with the goats. Now off you go."

It was very beautiful on the mountain that morning. The night wind had blown all the clouds away and the sky was deep blue. The sun shone brilliantly on the green pasture land and on the flowers which were blooming everywhere. There were primroses, blue gentian, and dainty yellow rock-roses. Heidi rushed to and fro, wild with excitement at sight of them. She quite forgot Peter and the goats, and kept stopping to gather flowers and put them in her apron. She wanted to take them home to stick among the hay in her bedroom, to make it look like a meadow.

Peter needed eyes all round his head. It was more than one pair could do to keep watch on Heidi as well as the goats, for they too were running about in all directions. He had to whistle and shout and swing his stick in the air to bring the wandering animals together.

"Where have you got to now, Heidi?" he called once rather crossly.

146

"Here," came her voice from behind a little hillock some distance back. It was covered with primulas which had a most delicious scent. Heidi had never smelled anything so lovely before and had sat down among them to enjoy it to the full.

"Come on," called Peter. "Uncle said I wasn't to let you fall over the ravine."

"Where's that?" she called, without moving.

"Right up above. We've still a long way to go, so do come on. Hear the old hawk croaking away up there?"

Heidi jumped up at this last remark and ran to him with her apron full of flowers.

"You've got enough now," he said, as they started to climb again. "Don't pick any more, otherwise you'll always be lagging behind, and besides, if you keep on, there won't be any left for tomorrow."

Heidi saw the sense of this, and anyway her apron was almost full. She kept close to Peter after that, and the goats went on in a more orderly fashion too, for now they could smell the fragrant herbs they loved which grew on their grazing ground, and were anxious to reach them.

"Come on," called Peter. "Uncle said I wasn't to let you fall over the ravine."

Peter usually took up his quarters for the day at the very foot of a rocky mountain peak. On the steep slopes above, there were only a few bushes and stunted fir trees, and the summit itself was just bare rock. On one side was the sheer drop over the ravine which Uncle Alp had spoken of. When they reached this place Peter took off his knapsack and laid it, for safety, in a little hollow, for there were sometimes strong gusts of wind and he had no wish to see his precious food go bowling down the mountain. Then he lay down in the sun to rest after the strenuous climb. Heidi put her apronful of flowers in the same little hollow. Then she sat down beside Peter and looked around her. The valley below was bathed in sunlight. In front of them a snowclad mountain stood out against the blue sky and to the left of this was a huge mass of rock, with jagged twin peaks. Everything was very still. Only a gentle breeze set the blue and yellow flowers nodding on their slender stems.

Peter fell asleep and the goats climbed about among the bushes. Heidi sat quite still, enjoying it all. She gazed so intently at the mountain peaks that soon they seemed to her to have faces and to be looking at her like old friends. Suddenly she heard a loud noise. Looking up, she saw an enormous bird, circling overhead with outstretched wings and croaking harshly as it flew. "Peter, Peter, wake up!" she cried. "Here's the hawk." Peter sat up and together they watched as the great bird soared higher and higher into the sky and finally disappeared over the grey peaks.

Only a gentle breeze set the blue and yellow flowers nodding on their slender stems.

"Where's it gone to?" asked Heidi, who had never seen a bird as big as that before and had watched its flight with great interest.

"Home to its nest," replied Peter.

"Does it live right up there? How wonderful! Why does it make such a noise?"

"Because it has to," explained Peter briefly.

"Let's climb up and see where it lives," she proposed.

148

"Oh, no, we won't! Even the goats can't climb as high as that, and don't forget Uncle told me to look after you," he said with marked disapproval. To Heidi's surprise he then began whistling and shouting, but the goats recognized the familiar sounds and came towards him from all directions, though some lingered to nibble a tasty blade of grass, while others butted one another playfully.

Heidi jumped up and ran among them, delighted to see them so obviously enjoying themselves. She spoke to each one, and every one was different and easily distinguishable from the others.

Meanwhile Peter opened his bag and spread its contents out in a square on the ground, two large portions for Heidi and two smaller ones for himself. Then he filled the mug with milk from Daisy and placed it in the middle of the square. He called to Heidi, but she was slower to come than the goats had been. She was so busy with her new playmates that she had ears and eyes for nothing else. He went on calling till his voice re-echoed from the rocks and at last she appeared. When she saw the meal laid out so invitingly, she skipped up and down with pleasure.

> When she saw the meal laid out so invitingly, she skipped up and down with pleasure.

"Stop jigging about," said Peter, "it's dinnertime. Sit down and begin."

"Is the milk for me?"

"Yes, and those huge pieces of bread and cheese. I'll get you another mugful from Daisy when you've drunk that one. Then I'll have a drink myself."

"Where will you get yours from?" she inquired.

149

"From my own goat, Spot. Now start eating."

She drank the milk, but ate only a small piece of bread and passed the rest over to Peter, with the cheese. "You can have that," she said. "I've had enough." He looked at her with amazement for he had never in his life had any food to give away. At first he hesitated, thinking she must be joking, but she went on holding it out to him and finally put it on his knee. This convinced him that she really meant what she said, so he took it, nodded his thanks and settled down to enjoy the feast. Heidi meanwhile sat watching the goats.

"What are they all called, Peter?" she asked presently.

Peter did not know a great deal, but this was a question he could answer without difficulty. He told her all the names, pointing to each animal in turn. She listened attentively and soon knew one from the other. Each had little tricks by which it could easily be recognized by anyone looking at them closely, as she was doing. Big Turk had strong horns, and was always trying to butt the others, so they kept out of his way as much

> "What's the matter, Snowflake? What are you crying for?"

as possible. The only one to answer him back was a frisky little kid called Finch, with sharp little horns, and Turk was generally too astonished at such impudence to make a fight of it. Heidi was particularly attracted to a little white goat called Snowflake, which was bleating most pitifully. She had tried earlier to comfort it. Now she ran up to it again, put her arm round its neck, and asked fondly, "What's the matter, Snowflake? What are you crying for?" At that, the goat nestled against her and stopped bleating.

Peter had not yet finished his meal, but he called out between mouthfuls, "She's crying because her mother doesn't come up here any more. She's been sold to someone in Mayenfeld."

"Where's her grandmother then?"

"Hasn't got one."

"Or her grandfather?"

"Hasn't one."

"Poor Snowflake," said Heidi, hugging the little animal again. "Don't cry any more. I shall be up here every day now, and you can always come to me if you feel lonely." Snowflake rubbed her head on the little girl's shoulder, and seemed to be comforted.

"Poor Snowflake," said Heidi, hugging the little animal again.

Peter had now finished eating, and came up to Heidi who was making fresh discoveries all the time. She noticed that Daisy and Dusky seemed more independent than the other goats and carried themselves with a sort of dignity. They led the way as the herd went up to the bushes again. Some of them stopped here and there to sample a tasty herb, others went straight up, leaping over any small obstacles in their path. Turk was up to his tricks as usual, but Daisy and Dusky ignored him completely and were soon nibbling daintily at the leaves of the two thickest bushes. Heidi watched them for some time. Then she turned to Peter, who was lying full length on the grass.

"Daisy and Dusky are the prettiest of all the goats," she said.

"I know. That's Uncle—he keeps them very clean and gives them salt and he

152

has a fine stall for them," he replied. Then he suddenly jumped up and ran after his herd, with Heidi close behind, anxious not to miss anything. He had noticed that inquisitive little Finch was right at the edge of the ravine, where the ground fell away so steeply that if it went any farther, it might go over and would certainly break its legs. Peter stretched out his hands to catch hold of the little kid, but he slipped and fell, though he managed to grasp one of its legs and Finch, highly indignant at such treatment, struggled wildly to get away. "Heidi, come here," called Peter, "come and help."

He couldn't get up unless he let go of Finch's leg which he was nearly pulling out of its socket already. Heidi saw at once what to do, and pulled up a handful of grass which she held under Finch's nose.

"Come on, don't be silly," she said. "You don't want to fall down there and hurt yourself."

At that the little goat turned round and ate the grass from her hand, and Peter was able to get up. He took hold of the cord, on which a little bell was hung round Finch's neck. Heidi took hold of it too, on the other side, and together they brought the runaway safely back to the herd. Then Peter took up his stick to give it a good beating, and seeing what was coming, Finch tried to get out of the way.

"Don't beat him," pleaded Heidi. "See how frightened he is."

"He deserves it," Peter replied, raising his arm, but she caught hold of him and exclaimed, "No, you're not to! It will hurt him. Leave him alone!" she looked at him so fiercely that he was astonished and dropped the stick.

"I won't beat him if you'll give me some of your cheese again tomorrow," he said, feeling he ought to have some compensation after the fright the little goat had given him.

"You can have it all, tomorrow and every day," promised Heidi, "I shan't want it. And I'll give you some of my bread as well, but then you must never beat Finch or Snowflake or any of them."

"It's all the same to me," said Peter, which was his way of saying that he promised. He let Finch go and it bounded back to the herd.

It was getting late and the setting sun spread a wonderful golden glow over the grass and the flowers, and the high peaks shone and sparkled. Heidi sat for while, quietly enjoying the beautiful scene, then all at

> "I won't beat him if you'll give me some of your cheese again tomorrow," he said, feeling he ought to have some compensation after the fright the little goat had given him.

154

once she jumped up, crying, "Peter, Peter! A fire, a fire! The mountains are on fire, and the snow and the sky too. Look, the trees and the rocks are all burning, even up there by the hawk's nest. Everything's on fire!"

"It's always like this in the evening," Peter said calmly, whittling away at his stick. "It's not a fire."

"What is it then?" she cried, rushing about to look at the wonderful sight from all sides. "What is it, Peter?"

"It just happens," he said.

"Oh, just see, the mountains have got all rosy red! Look at the one with the snow on it, and that one with the big rocks at the top. What are their names, Peter?"

"Mountains don't have names," he answered.

"Is it always like this up here?" asked Heidi hopefully.

"How pretty the rosy snow looks, and the red rocks. Oh dear," she added, after a pause, "now the color's going and everything's turning grey. Oh, it's all over." She sat down, looking as upset as if it was indeed the end of everything.

"It'll be the same again tomorrow," explained Peter. "Now it's time to go home." He whistled and called the goats together and they started the downward journey.

"Is it always like this up here?" asked Heidi hopefully.

"Usually."

"Will it really be the same tomorrow?"

"Yes, it will," he assured her.

Do You

Do you **carrot** all for me?

My heart **beets** for you,

With your **turnip** nose

And your **radish** face,

158

Carrot All For Me?

Anonymous

You are a peach.
If we cantaloupe,
Lettuce marry;
Weed make a swell pear.

Special Delivery

The next time you celebrate your best friend's birthday or your favorite holiday, take the time to do so with your own collection of signature stationery. Handmade letters are an easy way to send a little extra love in the mail, whether you're saying "Thanks" or simply "Thinking of you." All you need is plain or colored writing paper to start your stationery collection. Then try some of these ideas. Have fun!

Polka-dot Press

New pencil with eraser, ink pad

Decorate with dots! You can make perfect polka dot borders by pressing a pencil's new eraser on an ink pad. Then stamp dots around the edges of your paper.

Sparkle Art

Toothpicks, glue, glitter, paper plate

1. Dip the end of a toothpick in glue and draw decorative borders or write a fancy signature on your stationery.
2. Pour some glitter onto a paper plate. Sprinkle the glitter sparingly onto the wet glue on your paper. Leave to dry.
3. Hold up paper and tap excess glitter onto a paper plate for reuse.

Embossing

Scissors, cardboard, rice, toothpicks, string, waterproof glue, basin of water, sponge

Make your letterhead really stand out by embossing the top part of your stationery with your own design. Or emboss the front of a note card.

1. Cut a square of cardboard about the size of your notepaper.

2. Create designs such as flowers or animals by arranging kernels of rice or toothpicks on the cardboard. Or spell your name with string. Then glue the objects onto the cardboard and let the glue dry thoroughly.

3. Dip your notepaper in water and let it soak for a few seconds.

4. Carefully shake excess water from the paper and lay it onto the cardboard. Use the sponge to press the paper onto your design so that it appears raised. Let the paper dry completely before writing your letter.

Signed & Sealed

Pen, large rubber eraser, X-Acto knife, small candle

1. Use a pen to draw your initial on one side of an eraser—be sure to draw your initial backwards.

2. Ask an adult to help carve away everything but your initial.

3. With a lit candle (and adult supervision), carefully drip 8-12 drops of wax onto your envelope.

4. Press your initial into the wax before it cools.

Shower the People

by James Taylor

Shower the people you love with love; Show them the way that you feel. Things are gonna work out fine, If you only will. Shower the people you love with love; Show them the way you feel. Things are gonna be much better if you only will.

You can play the game and you can act out the part
Though you know it wasn't written for you.
But tell me how can you stand there with your broken heart
Ashamed of playing the fool.
One thing can lead to another;
It doesn't take any sacrifice.
Oh, father and mother, sister and brother,
If it feels nice don't think twice.

Just... (Chorus)

You can run but you cannot hide; ——
This is widely known.
And what you plan to do with your foolish pride
When you're all by yourself alone.
Once you tell somebody the way that you feel
You can feel it beginning to ease.
   I think it's true what they say about the squeaky wheel,
     Always getting the grease.

      Better to... (Chorus) *oh ho ho nn n*

       Shower the people you love with love;
       Show them the way that you feel.

Grandmas often know best when it comes to cookie recipes. That's why these sugar cookies are as good as they get. For a no-bake option, try the chilled oatmeal cookies. If you're in the mood for something chocolaty, be sure to try the Rocky Road Fudge or Chocolate Turtles. You'll see how Mississippi Mud Bars got their name when you swirl white and dark chocolate across the top! Yum!

Sweet Treats

Granny Eileen's World's Best Sugar Cookies

1 cup sugar
1 cup confectioner's sugar
2 eggs
1 cup oil
1 cup butter
1 teaspoon vanilla
5 cups flour
1 teaspoon baking soda
1 teaspoon cream of tartar
$1/4$ teaspoon salt

1. Preheat oven to 375°F.
2. Beat sugars, eggs, oil, butter, and vanilla until fluffy. Mix in flour, baking soda, cream of tartar, and salt.
3. Use a teaspoon to form dough into balls and drop onto a greased cookie sheet 2 inches apart. Press down on each cookie with the bottom of a glass.
4. Bake for 10 minutes until golden.
5. Transfer cookies to wire racks and let cool.

Makes approximately 7 dozen cookies.

No-Bake Oatmeal Cookies

2 cups sugar
$1/2$ cup milk
1 stick ($1/2$ cup) butter, softened to room temperature
3 cups quick oats
3 tablespoons cocoa powder
1 teaspoon vanilla
$3/4$ cup peanut butter

1. In a saucepan, mix sugar, milk, and butter. Bring to a boil, stirring frequently. Boil for one minute, then remove from heat.
OR:
Combine sugar, milk, and butter in microwavable bowl. Microwave on medium high in 1-minute intervals until melted, stirring in between timings.
2. In a large bowl, blend oats, cocoa powder, vanilla, and peanut butter into butter mixture.
3. Line a cookie sheet with wax paper. Use a teaspoon to drop balls of dough onto cookie sheet. Cover with plastic wrap and refrigerate overnight.

Makes about 3 dozen cookies.

Mississippi Mud Bars

1 stick (1/2 cup) butter, softened to
    room temperature
3/4 cup brown sugar
1 teaspoon vanilla
1 egg, room temperature
1 1/3 cup flour
1/2 teaspoon baking soda
1/4 teaspoon salt
1/2 cup pecans, chopped
1 cup chocolate chips
1 cup white chocolate chips

1. Preheat oven to 375°F.
2. In a large bowl, cream butter, sugar, and vanilla. Beat in egg until light and creamy.
3. Mix in flour, baking soda, and salt until blended. Fold in nuts, 3/4 cup chocolate chips, and 3/4 cup white chips.
4. Spread cookie-dough mixture evenly onto a greased 13- by 9-inch pan. Bake for 23 to 28 minutes, or until golden brown on top and center feels firm. Remove from oven and immediately sprinkle remaining chocolate and white chips on top, letting them melt.
5. Spread melted chips into swirls with a butter knife across top of pan cookie. Allow to cool before cutting into bars.

Makes 18 to 24 bars.

Rocky Road Fudge

12 ounces chocolate chips
2 tablespoons butter, softened to room temperature
14 ounces sweetened condensed milk
2 cups dry-roasted peanuts
10 1/2 ounces mini-marshmallows

1. Combine chocolate chips, butter, and condensed milk in a saucepan over low heat, stirring frequently. When melted, remove from heat and allow to cool for about 10 minutes.
2. In a large bowl, combine nuts and marshmallows. Add chocolate mixture and blend well.
3. Pour fudge mixture into a 13- by 9-inch pan and chill for at least 2 hours. Cut into small squares.

Makes 2 to 3 dozen pieces.

Chocolate Turtles

2 cups chocolate chips
1¹/4 sticks butter, softened to room temperature
14 ounces caramels
2 tablespoons milk
1 cup whole pecan halves

1. Line 8- by 11-inch pan with foil and set aside. In a small microwavable bowl, microwave 1 cup chocolate chips and ¹/8 stick (1 tablespoon) butter on medium high in 1-minute intervals until melted, stirring in between timings.
2. Pour mixture into foil-lined pan and refrigerate for 15 to 20 minutes.
3. In a medium-size microwavable bowl, melt caramels, 1 stick (¹/2 cup) butter, and milk on medium high in 1-minute intervals, stirring in between timings.
4. Stir in pecans and pour over chilled chocolate.
5. In a small microwavable bowl, melt remaining 1 cup chocolate chips and ¹/2 stick (1 tablespoon) butter on medium-high heat as in step 1.
6. Spread chocolate over caramel layer and refrigerate for 1 to 2 hours. Turn pan upside down onto cutting board and remove foil. Cut into 1-inch squares. Store in refrigerator.

Makes approximately 5 dozen turtles.

LARGEST COOKIE Made at the annual Riponfest in Ripon, WI, on July 11, 1992, the world's largest cookie was a chocolate chip cookie with a surface area of 907.9 feet. Measuring 34 feet in diameter, it had nearly 4 million chocolate chips.

Sweet Feats

LARGEST CANDY The distinction of largest candy goes to a marzipan chocolate weighing 4,078 pounds, 8 ounces. It was made at the Ven International Fresh Market in Diemen, Netherlands, on May 11–13, 1990.

LONGEST BANANA SPLIT On April 30, 1988, the residents of Selinsgrove, Pennsylvania, made the world's longest banana split as a fund-raising event for the local high school band. Stretching along Market Street, the split measured 4.55 miles in length. The feat also required the engineering of the world's longest continuous dish.

LARGEST BUBBLE-GUM BUBBLE Measured under the strict rules of the fiercely competitive activity of bubble-gum bubble blowing, the largest diameter for a bubble was 23 inches, by Susan Montgomery Williams of Fresno, CA, on July 19, 1994.

LARGEST CAKE Prepared by the EarthGrains bakery in Fort Payne, AL, the world's largest cake weighed in at 128,238 pounds, 8 ounces, including 16,209 pounds of icing. Made in the shape of Alabama, it was baked to commemorate the one hundredth birthday of Fort Payne. The first cut was made by fellow centenarian and resident Ed Henderson on October 18, 1989.

LARGEST MILKSHAKE Manhattan's Ira Freehof, who has the unique distinction of owning the celebrated Comfort Diners, also broke the record for world's largest milkshake on August 1, 2000, with a 6,000-gallon classic Black & White shake that shattered the previous record of 4,603.24 gallons.

You've Got a Friend

by Carole King

When you're down and troubled
And you need some love and care
And nothin', nothin' is goin' right,
Close your eyes and think of me
And soon I will be there
To brighten up even your darkest night.

(Chorus)

If the sky above you
Grows dark and full of clouds
And that ol' north wind begins to blow,
Keep your head together
And call my name out loud;
Soon you'll hear me knockin' at your door.

(Chorus)

Now ain't it good to know that you've got a friend
When people can be so cold?
They'll hurt you, yes, and desert you
And take your soul if you let them.
Oh, but don't you let them.

(Chorus)

You just call out my name and you know wherever I am I'll come runnin', to see you again. Winter, spring, summer or fall, all you have to do is call and I'll be there. You've got a friend.

Marilla and Matthew Cuthbert are getting on in years and need help on their Prince Edward Island farm, Green Gables. They decide to adopt a young boy, and are flabbergasted when the orphanage mistakenly sends skinny little Anne Shirley. Soon enough, however, eleven-year-old Anne's one-of-a-kind personality not only wins the hearts of her reluctant adoptive parents, but of the rest of the townspeople, too. Montogomery's heroine, with her perfect mix of brilliance, bullheadedness, and naïveté, moved Mark Twain—author of *The Adventures of Tom Sawyer* and *The Adventures of Huckleberry Finn*—to write that Anne was "the dearest, most lovable child in fiction since the immortal Alice" of *Alice's Adventures in Wonderland.* Like her charming creation, Anne Shirley, Lucy Maud Montgomery (1874-1942) lived on Prince Edward Island in Canada. In all, Montgomery penned eight books in the Green Gables series: *Anne of Green Gables* (1908), *Anne of Avonlea* (1909), *Anne of the Island* (1915), *Anne's House of Dreams* (1917), *Rainbow Valley* (1919), *Rilla of Ingleside* (1921), *Anne of Ingleside* (1936), and *Anne of Windy Poplars* (1939).

"What a splendid day!" said Anne, drawing a long breath. "Isn't it good just to be alive on a day like this? I pity the people who aren't born yet for missing it. They may have good days, of course, but they can never have this one. And it's splendider still to have such a lovely way to go to school by, isn't it?"

"It's a lot nicer than going round by the road; that is so dusty and hot," said Diana practically, peeping into her dinner basked and mentally calculating if the three juicy, toothsome, raspberry tarts reposing there were divided among ten girls how many bites each girl would have.

The little girls of Avonlea school always pooled their lunches, and to eat three raspberry tarts all alone or even to share them only with one's best chum would have forever and ever branded as "awful mean" the girl who did it. And yet, when the tarts were divided among ten girls you just got enough to tantalize you.

The way Anne and Diana went to school *was* a pretty one. Anne thought those walks to and from school with Diana couldn't be improved upon even by imagination. Going around by the main road would have been so unromantic; but to go by Lovers' Lane and Willowmere and Violet Vale and the Birch Path was romantic, if ever anything was.

Anne of Green Gables

by
L. M. Montgomery

173

Lovers' Lane opened out below the orchard at Green Gables and stretched far up into the woods to the end of the Cuthbert farm. It was the way by which the cows were taken to the back pasture and the wood hauled home in winter. Anne had named it Lovers' Lane before she had been a month at Green Gables.

"Not that lovers ever really walk there," she explained to Marilla, "but Diana and I are reading a perfectly magnificent book and there's a Lovers' Lane in it. So we want to have one, too. And it's a very pretty name, don't you think? So romantic! We can imagine the lovers into it, you know. I like that lane because you can think out loud there without people calling you crazy."

Anne, starting out alone in the morning, went down Lovers' Lane as far as the brook. Here Diana met her, and the two little girls went on up the lane under the leafy arch of maples—"maples are such sociable trees," said Anne; "they're always rustling and whispering to you,"—until they came to a rustic bridge. Then they left the lane and walked through Mr. Barry's back field and past Willowmere. Beyond Willowmere came Violet Vale—a little green dimple in the shadow of Mr. Andrew Bell's big woods. "Of course there are no violets there now," Anne told Marilla, "but Diana says there are millions of them in spring. Oh, Marilla, can't you just imagine you see them? It actually takes away my breath. I named it Violet Vale. Diana says she never saw the beat of me for hitting on fancy names for places. It's nice to be clever at something, isn't it? But Diana named the Birch Path. She wanted to, so I let her; but I'm sure I could have found something more poetical than plain Birch Path. Anybody can think of a name like that. But the Birch Path is one of the prettiest places in the world, Marilla."

It was. Other people besides Anne thought so when they stumbled on it. It

And how on earth would she ever manage to hold her tongue during school hours?

was a little narrow, twisting path, winding down over a long hill straight through Mr. Bell's woods, where the light came down sifted through so many emerald screens that it was as flawless as the heart of a diamond. It was fringed in all its length with slim young birches, white-stemmed and lissome boughed; ferns and starflowers and wild lilies-of-the-valley and scarlet tufts of pigeon berries grew thickly along it; and always there was a delightful spiciness in the air and music of bird calls and the murmur and laugh of wood winds in the trees overhead. Now and then you might see a rabbit skipping across the road if you were quiet— which, with Anne and Diana, happened about once in a blue moon. Down in the valley the path came out to the main road and then it was just up the spruce hill to the school.

The Avonlea school was a whitewashed building, low in the eaves and wide in the windows, furnished inside with comfortable substantial old-fashioned desks that opened and shut, and were carved all over their lids with the initials and hieroglyphics of three generations of schoolchildren. The schoolhouse was set back from the road and behind it was a dusky fir wood and a brook where all the children put their bottles of milk in the morning to keep cool and sweet until dinner hour.

Marilla had seen Anne start off to school on the first day of September with many secret misgivings. Anne was such an odd girl. How would she get on with the other children? And how on earth would she ever manage to hold her tongue during school hours?

Things went better than Marilla feared, however. Anne came home that evening in high spirits.

"I think I'm going to like school here," she announced. "I don't think much of the master, though. He's all the time curling his moustache and making eyes at Prissy Andrews. Prissy is grown up, you know. She's sixteen and she's studying for the entrance examination into Queen's Academy at Charlottetown next year. Tillie Boulter says the master is *dead gone* on her. She's got a beautiful complexion and curly brown hair and she does it up so elegantly. She sits in the long seat at the back and he sits there, too, most of the time—to explain her lessons, he says. But Ruby Gillis says she saw him writing something on her slate and when Prissy read it she blushed as red as a beet and giggled; and Ruby Gillis says she doesn't believe it had anything to do with the lesson."

"Anne Shirley, don't let me hear you talking about your teacher that way again," said Marilla sharply. "You don't go to school to criticize the master. I guess he can teach *you* something and it's your business to learn. And I want you to understand right off that you are not to come home telling tales about him. That is something I won't encourage. I hope you were a good girl."

"Indeed I was," said Anne comfortably. "It wasn't so hard as you might imagine, either. I sit with Diana.

"Anne Shirley, don't let me hear you talking about your teacher that way again."

Our seat is right by the window and we can look down to the Lake of Shining Waters. There are a lot of nice girls in school and we had scrumptious fun playing at dinner time. It's so nice to have a lot of little girls to play with. But of course I like Diana best and always will. I *adore* Diana. I'm dreadfully far behind the others. They're all in the fifth book and I'm only in the fourth. I feel that it's kind of a disgrace. But there's not one of them has such an imagination as I have and I soon found that out. We had reading and geography and Canadian History and dictation today. Mr. Phillips said my spelling was disgraceful and he held up my slate so that everybody could see it, all marked over. I felt so mortified, Marilla; he might have been politer to a stranger, I think. Ruby Gillis gave me an apple and Sophia Sloane lent me a lovely pink card with 'May I see you home?' on it. I'm to give it back to her tomorrow. And Tillie Boulter let me wear her bead ring all the afternoon. Can I have some of those pearl beads off the old pincushion in the garret to make myself a ring? And oh Marilla, Jane Andrews told me that Minnie MacPherson told her that she heard Prissy Andrews tell Sara Gillis that I had a very pretty nose. Marilla, that is the first compliment I have ever had in my life and you can't imagine what a strange feeling it gave me. Marilla, have I really a pretty nose? I know you'll tell me the truth."

"Your nose is well enough," said Marilla shortly. Secretly she thought Anne's nose was a remarkably pretty one; but she had no intention of telling her so.

That was three weeks ago and all had gone smoothly so far. And now, this crisp September morning, Anne and Diana were tripping blithely down the Birch Path, two of the happiest little girls in Avonlea.

Nature Stencils

Y ou don't have to be a masterful artist to be able to make prints like one. You can easily trace shapes that you like onto heavy paper, cut them out, and have an instant stencil. Look for flowers or feathers in your backyard, sand dollars or seashells on the beach, or leaves and seedpods in wooded areas. Then you can transfer your artistic motifs onto jewelry boxes, wallpaper borders, book covers, stationery, wrapping paper, or just about anything you'd like to paint.

Scissors, manila folders, pencil, ruler, masking tape, paint, paper plate, stencil brushes

1. Start by collecting items that you can easily trace.
2. Cut a manila folder in half along the spine. Arrange a few objects on one of the halves and trace their outlines.
3. Cut out your patterns as "holes" in the folder. Try to be as exact as possible. The crisper you can keep the edges as you cut, the sharper your stencils will appear.
4. Decide what you want to stencil. If you'd like to transfer a repeated motif, you can use a ruler to draw a faint borderline on the surface you're stenciling to use as a reference line. Then position the stencil where the pattern should begin and tape it in place with masking tape.
5. Pour some paint onto a paper plate. A secret to good stenciling is not to use too much paint at a time. Dip your brush in the paint and blot excess paint onto the paper plate. Carefully dab the brush onto the surface that you wish to paint. Start along the edges of the stencil and work your way into the middle.
6. Let the paint dry before removing the stencil pattern and taping it into a new position. Repeat the steps until you have completed the entire area you want to stencil. What an impressionist!

IDIOMS

An idiom is a figurative expression, used in a particular language, that only makes sense within the context of its entire sentence.

Eyes in the back of your head To have eyes in the back of your head means that you seem to know what happens even when your back is turned or when you're not around.

Spill the beans To spill the beans means to tell a secret to someone who is not supposed to know about it.

Eat your words To eat your words means to take back something you said or to admit you have been proven wrong.

At the drop of a hat To do something at the drop of a hat means to do it without waiting, immediately, promptly.

By word of mouth "I heard the news by word of mouth" means that you are not being specific about whose mouth you heard it from; just that you heard it from another person.

Stick your neck out To stick your neck out means to do something dangerous or risky for someone.

What do these idioms mean?

- Any Tom, Dick or Harry • Right off the bat • Run rings around somebody •
- Cut and dry • Few and far between • Have a soft spot • Spread like wildfire •
- Something smells fishy • Make or break • Head over heels •
- Not my cup of tea • Start from scratch • You're skating on thin ice •
- It's in the bag • Hold your tongue • Time flies • Hit the roof •
- Out of the blue • Sweet tooth • Know something like the back of your hand •

PALINDROMES

A palindrome is a word that is spelled the same way backward and forward:

civic	madam	radar
dad	mom	refer
deed	noon	reviver
did	nun	rotor
eve	peep	stats
ewe	pop	tat
eye	pullup	toot
kayak	pup	tot
level	racecar	wow

Can you create a sentence that is a palindrome? These sentence can be read backwards and forwards. Here's are some examples:

> Was it a car or a cat I saw?
>
> Step on no pets.
>
> Marge lets Norah see Sharon's telegram.
>
> Never odd or even.
>
> Too bad, I hid a boot.

One of the most famous palindromes is "A man, a plan, a canal—Panama!" by Leigh Mercer, 1914.

Word Fun!

All in
Together Girls

All in together girls.
it's fine weather girls.
When is your birthday?
Please jump in.

(jump in on birthday)

January, February, March,
April, May, June, July,
August, September, October,
November, December.

All in together girls.
It's fine weather girls.
When is your birthday?
Please jump out.

*(say months again; jump out
on birthday)*

More

186

Jumpin' Rope

Geography Jump Rope

I took a trip around the world,
And this is where I went:
  From Asia to Boston;
  From Boston to Canada;
  From Canada to Denver
  From Denver to England—

(and so forth down the alphabet as long as the skipper can keep thinking of places—or until he/she misses)

Down in the Valley

Down in the valley where the
  green grass grows,
There sat *(name of jumper)* as
  sweet as a rose,
She sang and she sang and
  she sang so sweet,
Along came *(name of boy)* and
  kissed her on the cheek.
How many kisses did she get?
1, 2, 3, 4, 5, 6, 7. . .

In Time of Silver Rain

by Langston Hughes

In time of silver rain
The **earth**
Puts forth new life again,
Green grasses grow
And flowers lift their heads,
And over all the plain
The **wonder** spreads
Of life,
Of life,
Of life!

In time of silver rain
The **butterflies**
Lift silken wings
To catch a rainbow cry,
And trees put forth
New leaves to **sing**

In **joy** beneath the sky
As down the roadway
Passing boys and girls
Go singing, too,
In time of silver rain
When spring
And life
Are new.

You Are So Beautiful To Me

by Billy Preston and Bruce Fisher

You are so beautiful to me.
You are so beautiful to me.
Can't you see
You're everything that I hope for and what's more,
You're everything I need.
You are so beautiful baby to me.

Such joy and happiness you bring.
I wanna thank you babe.
Such joy and happiness you bring, just like a dream.
You're like a guiding light shinin' in the night,
You're heaven still to me.
Hey babe,
You Are So Beautiful.

Appliqué Art

*D*on't throw that old shirt away! Cut it up and turn it into jazzy patchwork for your jeans, book bags, or jackets. Add some pizazz with rhinestones and ribbon. The art of appliqué is sewing one piece of fabric onto another to make fun or eccentric designs. Start collecting notions and fabric scraps of different colors and textures. Then see what you can stitch together.

Tracing paper, pencil, measuring tape, pins, fabric, scissors, fabric glue, needle, thread, sequins, rhinestones, and other notions, an adult with a sewing machine (optional!)

1. Create a pattern. You may want to start with simple forms such as stars, hearts, moons, or diamonds. You can also combine shapes to make animals, fruit, faces, flowers…whatever! For fresh ideas, try looking in magazines and cutting out pictures that will be easy to trace.

2. Draw your designs on separate sheets of tracing paper. Use a measuring tape to mark a 1/4-inch margin around the outside of each pattern.

3. Pin each pattern onto the swatches of fabric you want to include in your appliqué. Cut along the outer line of your shape.

This will allow you to turn the edges under so that they won't fray. Remove your patterns and save them for reuse.

4. Layer and arrange the cut pieces of fabric the way you like. Gently turn under the edges of the material and pin or glue into place. Your appliqué is ready to be sewn together.

5. If you are using a needle and thread, stitch around the edges of each top layer of fabric, sewing it onto the swatch beneath it. If an adult is helping out with a sewing machine, a decorative zigzag stitch will do the trick. If you are using fabric glue, dab a little glue to attach each swatch of fabric to the layer beneath it.

6. Decide where to put your appliqué. Then pin it where you want it and sew or glue it in place!

*Here are some easy ideas to
get you started:*

ORANGE SLICE
Bottom layer: circle. *Middle layer*: circle
that's about $1/4$-inch smaller in diameter
than the bottom circle. *Top layer*: six
small pie-shaped slices.

CAT
Bottom layer: circle. *Middle layer*: two
medium-sized triangles (for ears), one
small triangle (for nose), two ovals (for
eyes). *Top layer*: two thin strips (for
pupils), ribbon or yarn for whiskers.

FLOWER
Bottom layer: circle. *Middle layer*: six hearts
arranged so that the points come together
in the center. *Top layer*: star in the center.

Questions

1 Cleopatra was the queen of which country?
- A. Egypt
- B. Italy
- C. Greece
- D. Syria
- E. Luxembourg

2 In *Harry Potter and the Sorcerer's Stone*, what is the name of the three-headed dog that protects the stone?
- A. Margaret
- B. Fluffy
- C. Wully
- D. Bully
- E. Snoopy

3 Which of these animals can run the fastest in the shortest period of time?
- A. Grizzly bear
- B. Cheetah
- C. Woodchuck
- D. Dog
- E. Chicken

4 What is the distinguishing feature of Wonder Woman's jet airplane?
- A. It's purple with pink polka dots
- B. It's made of kryptonite
- C. It's invisible
- D. It has no wings
- E. It can travel through time

5 Which set of numbers is NOT in the correct sequence?
- A. 42, 46, 48, 50, 52
- B. 11, 13, 15, 17, 19, 21
- C. 18, 15, 12, 9, 6, 3
- D. 0, 5, 10, 15, 20, 25, 30
- E. 15, 30, 45, 90, 135, 270, 405

✗ Answers

Test Yourself!

6 **Who sewed the first American flag?**
A. Mrs. Smith
B. Martha Stewart
C. Betty Crocker
D. Betsy Ross
E. Abigail Adams

7 **Which term represents a 0 score in tennis?**
A. Nada
B. Grand slam
C. Love
D. Deuce
E. Zilch

8 **How old is Barbie?**

A. She's in her teens.
B. She's in her 40s.
C. She's 100 years old.
D. She's in her 20s.
E. She's over 100 years old.

9 **How many flowers must a bee visit to make a spoonful of honey?**
A. 10
B. 400
C. 5,000
D. 10,000
E. 176

10 **Who was the president of the United States during the Civil War?**
A. Abraham Lincoln
B. Ulysses S. Grant
C. George Washington
D. Millard Fillmore
E. James Buchanan

Answers: 1: A; 2: B; 3: B; 4: C; 5: A; 6: D; 7: C; 8: B; 9: D; 10: A.

Thirst Quenchers

These festive and fruity beverages will help you beat the summer heat and buffer the winter winds! Sherbet Fizz, Sunset Coolers and Orange Tea Punch are perfect front-porch drinks. A smoothie can be a meal at breakfast or a super after-school treat. Experiment with different fruit and yogurt combinations in similar quantities to create your own fun flavors. Zesty Tomato Marys are delicious for weekend brunches, while mulled apple cider will add a little spice to a chilly afternoon.

Sherbet Fizz

8 ounces orange juice
1 20-ounce can of chunk pineapple with juice
16 ounces (2 cups) lemon sherbet
12 ounces ginger ale
8 strawberries

1. Combine orange juice, pineapple, and sherbet in a blender and whir until smooth. Pour into a large pitcher.
2. Add ginger ale to pitcher and stir with a wooden spoon.
3. To make strawberry garnishes, first remove stems. Make four to six deep cuts about $1/2$ inch from the top. Twist the strawberries slightly so that they spread out like fans. Place a strawberry fan on top of each drink or on the rim of the glass and serve.

Makes 8 servings.

Sunset Cooler

12 ounces grape juice
12 ounces orange juice
12 ounces pineapple juice
1 lime
6 teaspoons grenadine syrup

1. Pour grape juice into ice cube trays and freeze for about 2 hours or until hard.
2. In a large pitcher, combine orange and pineapple juice and stir with a wooden spoon.
3. Wash lime and cut into thin slices.
4. Pour orange-pineapple juice evenly into four glasses. Drop $1^1/2$ teaspoons grenadine into each glass (the syrup will settle to the bottom).
5. Add two or three grape ice cubes to each glass. Top drinks off with a few lime slices. Serve with straws.

Makes 4 servings.

Orange Tea Punch

2 cups water
4 black tea bags
2 cups orange juice
1 1/2 tablespoons sugar
2 cinnamon sticks
12 whole cloves
20 ounces ginger ale
orange slices

1. In a kettle or hot pot, bring water to boil. Pour boiling water into a 2-quart heatproof pitcher and add tea bags. Allow tea to steep for 4 to 6 minutes, or until as strong as desired. Remove tea bags.
2. In medium saucepan, combine orange juice, sugar, cinnamon sticks, and cloves. Bring to a boil, then lower heat and cover. Simmer for an additional 5 minutes.
3. Add the orange juice mixture to the tea. Cover and refrigerate overnight.
4. Strain tea into a punchbowl and add ginger ale. Ladle into glasses and serve with orange slices.

Makes 12 servings.

Very Berry Smoothie

1 cup milk
1 cup boysenberry yogurt
2/3 cup frozen raspberries
2/3 cup strawberries, fresh or frozen
1/4 teaspoon almond extract
4 ice cubes

Combine all ingredients in a blender and mix until smooth and frothy. Pour into glasses and serve immediately.

Makes 2 servings.

Icy Melon Smoothie

1 cup milk
1/2 cup vanilla yogurt
1 cup diced cantaloupe
1 nectarine, pitted
1 tablespoon honey
1/4 cup lemon juice
6 ice cubes

Combine all ingredients in a blender and mix until smooth. Pour into glasses and serve.

Makes 4 servings

Orange-Yogurt Smoothie

1 cup orange juice
1 cup vanilla yogurt
$^1/_2$ banana
4 ice cubes

Combine all ingredients in a blender and mix until smooth. Pour into glasses and serve.

Makes 2 servings.

Zesty Tomato Mary

3 tomatoes, peeled and diced
$^1/_2$ green bell pepper, chopped
$^1/_2$ cucumber, peeled and sliced
1 tablespoon lemon juice
$^1/_2$ teaspoon horseradish
$^1/_4$ teaspoon dill weed
dash salt
3–4 dashes red pepper sauce
5–6 ice cubes

Combine all ingredients in a blender and mix until smooth. Pour into glasses and serve.

Makes 4 servings.

Mulled Apple Cider

5 cups apple cider
6 cinnamon sticks
6 allspice berries
6 whole cloves
6 cardamom seeds
2 strips orange peel, about 4 inches long
   by 1 inch wide

1. In a medium saucepan, bring the apple cider, two cinnamon sticks, allspice berries, cloves, cardamom seeds and orange peel to a boil. Turn heat down to low and cover. Allow cider mixture to simmer for 15 minutes.
2. Pour cider through a strainer into mugs and garnish with additional cinnamon sticks.
3. Serve warm.

Makes 4 servings.

Eleven-year-old Francie Nolan lives in a tenement with her immigrant parents and her brother, Neeley, in the depressed section of Williamsburg, Brooklyn. Francie's pragmatic mother diligently works to put food on the table and provide a roof over her children's heads, while her dreamer husband is rarely sober or gainfully employed. But though these strains weigh heavy on her family, Francie clings to her childhood dreams. She is a fervent reader, devouring every book on her school library's shelves. There is no better joy in her world than snuggling up with a book on the fire escape—her tree so close that she feels as if she is nestled in its branches. Betty Smith (1896-1972) was born Elizabeth Wehmer to poor German-immigrant parents. *A Tree Grows in Brooklyn* (1943) is reminiscent of her life story. Like her heroine, Francie, Smith grew up in Brooklyn. She was forced to leave school with only an eighth-grade education to work in the factories. After marrying and raising two daughters, Smith determinedly completed her education. Though best known for her coming-of-age masterpiece, Smith also wrote three other novels, *Tomorrow Will Be Better* (1947), *Maggie-Now* (1958), and *Joy in the Morning* (1963), and several plays.

The library was a little old shabby place. Francie thought it was beautiful. The feeling she had about it was as good as the feeling she had about church. She pushed open the door and went in. She liked the combined smell of worn leather bindings, library paste and freshly-inked stamping pads better than she liked the smell of burning incense at high mass.

Francie thought that all the books in the world were in the library and she had a plan about reading all the books in the world. She was reading a book a day in alphabetical order and not skipping the dry ones. She remembered that the first author had been Abbott. She had been reading a book a day for a long time now and she was still in the B's. Already she had read about bees and buffalos, Bermuda vacations and Byzantine architecture. For all of her enthusiasm, she had to admit that some of the B's had been hard going. But Francie was a reader. She read everything she could find: trash, classics, time tables and the grocer's price list. Some of the reading had been wonderful; the Louisa Alcott books for example. She planned to read all the books over again when she had finished with the Z's.

Saturdays were different. She treated herself by reading a book not in the alphabetical sequence. On that day she asked the librarian to recommend a book.

A Tree Grows in Brooklyn

by

Betty Smith

After Francie had come in and closed the door quietly behind her—the way you were supposed to do in the library—she looked quickly at the little golden-brown pottery jug which stood at the end of the librarian's desk. It was a season indicator. In the fall it held a few sprigs of bittersweet and at Christmas time it held holly. She knew spring was coming, even if there was snow on the ground, when she saw pussy willow in the bowl. And today, on this summer Saturday of 1912, what was the bowl holding? She moved her eyes slowly up the jug past the thin green stems and little round leaves and saw . . . nasturtiums! Red, yellow, gold and ivory-white. A head pain caught her between the eyes at the taking in of such a wonderful sight. It was something to be remembered all her life.

"When I get big," she thought, "I will have such a brown bowl and in hot August there will be nasturtiums in it."

> "When I get big," she thought, "I will have such a brown bowl and in hot August there will be nasturtiums in it."

She put her hand on the edge of the polished desk liking the way it felt. She looked at the neat row of freshly-sharpened pencils, the clean green square of blotter, the fat white jar of creamy paste, the precise stack of cards and the returned books waiting to be put back on the shelves. The remarkable pencil with the date slug above its point was by itself near the blotter's edge.

"Yes, when I get big and have my own home, no plush chairs and lace curtains for me. And *no* rubber plants. I'll have a desk like this in my parlor and white walls and a clean green blotter every Saturday night and a row of shining yellow pencils always sharpened for writing and a golden-brown bowl with a flower or some leaves or berries always in it and books . . . books. . .books. . ."

She chose her book for Sunday; something by an author named Brown. Francie figured she had been reading on the Brown's for months. When she thought she was nearly finished, she noticed that the next shelf started up again with Browne. After that Came Browning. She groaned, anxious to get into the C's where there was a book by Marie Corelli that she had peeped into and found thrilling. Would she *ever* get to that? Maybe she ought to read two books a day. Maybe. . . .

She stood at the desk a long time before the librarian deigned to attend to her.

"Yes?" inquired that lady pettishly.

"This book. I want it." Francie pushed the book forward opened at the back with the little card pushed out of the envelope. The librarians had trained the children to present the books that way. It saved them the trouble of opening several hundred books a day and pulling several hundred cards from as many envelopes.

She took the card, stamped it, pushed it down a slot in the desk. She stamped Francie's card and pushed it at her. Francie picked it up but she did not go away.

"Yes?" The librarian did not bother to look up.

"Could you recommend a good book for a girl?"

"Yes?" inquired that lady pettishly. "This book. I want it."

"How old?"

"She is eleven."

Each week Francie made the same request and each week the librarian asked the same question. A name on a card meant nothing to her and since she never looked up into a child's face, she never did get to know the little girl who took a book out every day and two on Saturday. A smile would have meant a lot to Francie and a friendly comment would have made her so happy. She loved the library and was anxious to worship the lady in charge. But the librarian had other things on her mind. She hated children anyhow.

Francie trembled in anticipation as the woman reached under the desk. She saw the title as the book came up: *If I Were King* by McCarthy. Wonderful! Last week it had been *Beverly of Graustark* and the same two weeks before that. She had had the McCarthy book only twice. The librarian recommended these two books over and over again. Maybe they were the only ones she herself had read; maybe they were on a recommended list; maybe she had discovered that they were sure fire as far as eleven-year-old girls were concerned.

Francine held the books close and hurried home, resisting the temptation to sit on the first stoop she came to, to start reading.

> Francine held the books close and hurried home, resisting the temptation to sit on the first stoop she came to, to start reading.

Home at last and now it was the time she had been looking forward to all week: fire-escape-sitting time. She put a small rug on the fire escape and got the pillow from her bed and propped it against the bars. Luckily there was ice in the icebox. She chipped off a small piece and put it in a glass of water. The pink-and-white peppermint wafers bought that morning were arranged in a little bowl, cracked, but of a pretty blue color. She arranged glass, bowl and book on the window sill and climbed out on the fire escape. Once out there, she was living in a tree. No one upstairs, downstairs or across the way could see her. But she could look out through the leaves and see everything.

> Once out there, she was living in a tree. No one upstairs, downstairs or across the way could see her. But she could look out through the leaves and see everything.

It was a sunny afternoon. A lazy warm wind carried a warm sea smell. The leaves of the tree made fugitive patterns on the white pillow case. Nobody was in the yard and that was nice. Usually it was pre-empted by the boy whose father rented the store on the ground floor. The boy played an interminable game of graveyard. He dug miniature graves, put live captured caterpillars into little match boxes, buried them with informal ceremony and erected little pebble headstones over the tiny earth mounds. The whole game was accompanied by fake sobbings and heavings of his chest. But today the dismal boy was away visiting an aunt in

Bensonhurst. To know that he was away was almost as good as getting a birthday present.

Francie breathed the warm air, watched the dancing leaf shadows, ate the candy and took sips of the cooled water in between reading the book.

> If I were King, Love,
> Ah, if I were King. . . .

The story of François Villon was more wonderful each time she read it. Sometimes she worried for fear the book would be lost in the library and she'd never be able to read it again. She had once started copying the book in a two-cent notebook. She wanted to own a book so badly and she had thought the copying would do it. But the penciled sheets did not seem like nor smell like the library book so she had given it up, consoling herself with the vow that when she grew up, she would work hard, save money and buy every single book that she liked.

As she read, at peace with the world and happy as only a little girl could be with a fine book and a little bowl of candy, and all alone in the house, the leaf shadows shifted and the afternoon passed.

MUST-READ BOOKS

In addition to the favorite titles excerpted in this book, here are other well-loved stories to add to your reading list. Happy reading!

BABE, THE GALLANT PIG by Dick King-Smith

A piglet destined to be butchered arrives at the barnyard, is adopted by an old sheep dog, and discovers a special secret to success.

BRIDGE TO TERABITHIA by Katherine Paterson

When his best friend drowns in the creek that surrounds their secret place in the woods, a young boy is left to come to terms with her death. 1978 Newbery Award.

CHARLOTTE'S WEB by E. B. White

The story of a little girl named Fern who loves a little pig named Wilbur and of Wilbur's dear friend, Charlotte A. Cavatica, a beautiful, large gray spider who lives with Wilbur in the barn.

THE DIARY OF A YOUNG GIRL by Anne Frank

The secret journal of a Dutch Jewish girl written during the time her family went into hiding from the Nazis during World War II.

FROM THE MIXED-UP FILES OF MRS. BASIL E. FRANKWEILER
by E. L. Konigsburg
A 12-year-old girl and her brother run away to the New York Metropolitan Museum of Art. 1968 Newbery Award.

THE INCREDIBLE JOURNEY by Sheila Burnford
Two dogs and a cat support each other through hardships, hunger, and danger as they travel 250 miles across Canada to reach home.

JULIE OF THE WOLVES by Jean Craighead George
While running away from home and an unwanted marriage, a 13-year-old Eskimo girl becomes lost on the North Slope of Alaska and befriends a wolf pack. 1973 Newbery Award.

A LITTLE PRINCESS by Frances Hodgson Burnett
Once the envy of all of her fellow students, a 7-year-old girl suddenly finds herself in the middle of a great tragedy, and has to learn how to cope and live again.

MARY POPPINS by P. L. Travers
The Banks children only expected the worst from their terribly proper and always prim nanny, but after seeing her slide up the banister, even a trip out the front door becomes an adventure.

MUST-READ BOOKS

MRS. FRISBY AND THE RATS OF NIMH by Robert O'Brien

In need of help for her children, a widowed mouse visits the rats whose former imprisonment in a laboratory has given them wisdom. A beautiful story about love and loyalty. 1972 Newbery Award.

RAMONA QUIMBY, AGE 8 by Beverly Cleary

Ramona's third-grade year at school will keep young readers laughing. A Newbery Honor book.

THE SECRET OF THE OLD CLOCK, NANCY DREW MYSTERY STORIES, NO. 1 by Carolyn M. Keene

Armed only with her sharp wits and detective instincts, Nancy Drew is on the case! In this story she searches for a missing will.

TUCK EVERLASTING by Natalie Babbitt

The Tuck family is confronted with an agonizing situation when they discover that a 10-year-old girl and a malicious stranger now share their secret about a spring whose water prevents one from ever growing any older.

A WRINKLE IN TIME by Madeline L'Engle

A trio of whimsical characters, intent on helping Meg find her father, take her, her brother, and a friend on an outer space voyage to a distant planet where an omnipotent brain has robotized everyone. 1963 Newbery Award.

No one has ever achieved anything from the smallest to the greatest unless the dream was dreamed first.

—LAURA INGALLS WILDER

MAYA ANGELOU (b. 1928) might be most famous for her poetry, but she has done much more than that. She has been a newspaper and magazine editor, and was a friend and colleague of Martin Luther King, Jr. Her book *I Know Why the Caged Bird Sings* made her one of the first African-American women on the bestseller list. Angelou also has been an actress, a singer, a director, a screenwriter, and a civil rights activist. And in 1993, President Clinton asked her to write and read a poem at his inauguration. Few people can claim as many accomplishments.

JANE AUSTEN (1775–1817) didn't have a lot of formal education and was pretty much taught to just draw and play the piano. But she did have access to her father's library of over five hundred volumes, and so she read a lot. Jane wrote her first book at 14, and went on to produce some of the best and most famous novels in the English language. Her books *Pride and Prejudice*, *Sense and Sensibility*, and *Emma* contain some of the strongest and smartest heroines in all literature.

MARGARET BOURKE-WHITE (1904–71) was one of the original photographers for *Life* and *Fortune* magazines during a period when there were few women doing this job. At first she was interested in only art and form; but then she started to take photos that were about social issues, like the problems of the poor and the homeless. Bourke-White became the first female photographer for the U.S. Army Air Corps and went to the front lines of World War II and the Korean Conflict.

ELLA FITZGERALD (1917–96) ran away from home at 16 and was living on the streets. To make money, she entered a talent contest at the famous Apollo Theater in Harlem and won first prize for singing. Someone in the audience then introduced her to a bandleader who gave Ella her first break. She eventually went on to be the favorite singer of many bandleaders and composers, and became known for her ability to sing all kinds of music. Many consider Fitzgerald to be the finest jazz singer who ever lived.

MARTHA GRAHAM (1894–1991) had a psychologist father who was very interested in the way people moved their bodies. This made an impression on her, and she grew up to study dancing. Graham lived in Greenwich Village in New York in the 1920s and 1930s and was exposed to many new forms of art and music, which she incorporated into her work. Unlike the traditional choreographers of the time, she created movement that was angular and didn't always flow smoothly. She is considered the mother of modern dance.

GEORGIA O'KEEFFE (1887–1986) knew in the eighth grade that she wanted to be an artist. All the women in her family were educated, and so Georgia attended art school. In 1916, a friend showed her drawings to Alfred Stieglitz, a famous photographer, who immediately put them up in his own gallery. From then, O'Keeffe became a successful artist who eventually spent much of her time in the New Mexico desert, expressing her uniquely powerful interpretations of flowers, bones, hills, and clouds.

Good Fortune

Can you really hold the future in your hands or see it in a teacup? For centuries people have believed that divination was possible by interpreting the tiny lines in the palm, tea-leaf patterns, or the way a stone on a string might swing. The practiced fortune-teller knows how such things reveal insights about life, love, health, and future events. Take a look for yourself. What do you see?

Palm Reading

Palmists look at the shape of the palm and fingers, the fleshy and hollow parts of the hand, fingernails, and skin texture. The most telling features of a person's palm, however, are the major lines.

Clearly defined lines = simplicity and ease
Crosshatches = difficulties or problems
A break in the line = dramatic change or illness
Deep or red lines = strong emotions

THE LIFE LINE starts between the thumb and index finger and outlines the base of the thumb. It tells about a person's health and longevity.

THE HEART LINE shows how affectionate a person is as well as how they fare in romance. It starts underneath the pinky finger and runs along the top of the palm toward the index finger.

THE HEAD LINE reveals a person's intelligence and mental capabilities. It starts underneath the index finger and runs underneath the heart line.

THE FORTUNE LINE runs straight up the center of the palm. It can indicate how strong a role fate plays in one's life. A weak line means that a person shapes her own future.

Tea Leaves

The next time you brew a cup of tea, use loose tea leaves. When you're down to the last few sips, concentrate on a question and swirl the leaves in your cup three times clockwise. Turn the cup upside down and drain the remaining tea into your saucer. After a few moments, turn the cup right side up and study the shapes and patterns. Tea leaves near the edge of the cup show what will happen soon; those near the bottom of the cup represent events in the distant future.

Airplane = journey
Angel = good news
Ant = hard work
Arrow = bad news
Bell = wedding
Bird = important news
Capital letter = first initial of someone
    you will meet

Cat = argument
Circle = success
Flowers = children
Kangaroo = harmony
Moon = romance
Rowboat = be patient
Snake = threat
Star = good luck
Tree = good health
Wheel = inheritance

The Pendulum

One of the easiest ways to tell fortunes is with a pendulum. It was common for people to learn the sex of unborn babies by holding a pendulum over a pregnant woman's abdomen. If it started swinging back and forth, the baby would be a boy. A circular swing indicated a girl.

Simply tie a small, weighty object, such as a ring or a key, to the end of a cord. Hold the end of the cord between two fingers and let the pendulum hang as still as possible. Ask a question for which you know the answer is definitely yes. Notice how the pendulum swings. Then ask a question for which you know the answer is definitely no. Watch how the pendulum changes direction. Once you get the swing of it, you'll be ready to find the answers to all kinds of yes or no questions.

Tomorrow, tomorrow
I love ya tomorrow
you're always a
day away!

Tomorrow

by Charles Strouse

The sun'll come out tomorrow
Bet your bottom dollar that tomorrow
There'll be sun!

Jus' thinking about tomorrow
Clears away the cobwebs and the sorrow
Till there's none.

When I'm stuck with a day that's gray and lonely,
I just stick out my chin and grin and say:

Oh! the sun'll come out tomorrow
So you got to hang on till tomorrow
Come what may!

Tomorrow, tomorrow, I love ya tomorrow,
You're always a day away.

Tomorrow, tomorrow, I love ya tomorrow,
You're always a day away.

WORD ORIGINS

*T*here are close to one million words in the English language, almost all of which began their lives as something else. Many are from foreign languages, like kayak *and* igloo, *from Inuit, and* shampoo *and* pajamas, *from Hindi. Take a look at some of the other words that have come to us from around the globe:*

ARABIC alcohol, algebra, candy, coffee, cotton, lemon, spinach, zero

CZECH robot

DUTCH cookie, coleslaw, dock, boss, pump

FRENCH art, beef, biscuit, boulevard, café, city, congress, constitution, court, curfew, dance, denim, essay, fashion, forest, medicine, mayonnaise, nation, omelette, rich, travel, umpire

GERMAN book, freedom, hamburger, husband, kindergarten, old, pretzel, queen, right, silly, work

GREEK alphabet, camp, cider, circus, gymnasium, museum, paper, paragraph, perfume, school, stomach, sugar

ITALIAN ballot, balloon, cantaloupe, chapel, piano, pizza, tarantula, volcano

LATIN asparagus, asthma, claim, hospital, legislator, library, mile, money, muscle, nice, pay, trivia, umbrella

NORWEGIAN egg, knife, ski, sky

SPANISH canyon, chocolate, cigar, mosquito, rodeo, tornado

SANSKRIT jungle, orange

TURKISH yogurt

CHINESE
ketchup,
tea

ACRONYMS

What is SCUBA? It's self-contained underwater-breathing apparatus. It is an acronym, a word made from the initial letters of words of a phrase. Acronyms become so familiar to us that we forget they originated with words. Do you know these common acronyms?

AWOL
(Absent Without Leave;
Absent Without Official Leave)

LASER
(Light Amplification by Stimulated
Emission of Radiation)

PIN
(Personal Identification Number)

RADAR
(Radio Detection and Ranging)

NASA
(National Aeronautics and
Space Administration)

Create your own acronyms to help you remember things. Here's two to start:

HOMES (Huron, Ontario, Michigan, Erie, and Superior): the Great Lakes

ROY G. BIV (Red, Orange, Yellow, Green, Blue, Indigo, Violet): the colors of the light spectrum

Word Fun!

223

Yummy Munchies

Whether you're having a slumber party or
an at-home movie night, you can
make the event more festive with
your own party snacks. Freshly
made potato and corn chips
taste amazing right out of the
oven—just right for sinking
into Seven-Layer Dip. It's so
easy to jazz up plain popcorn with flavors you
probably already have
in your cupboard or on
the spice rack. Don't
forget, veggies and nuts
can sometimes satisfy
a craving for
munchies too—and
they are healthy!

Tortilla Chips

1 dozen 6-inch corn tortillas, quartered
2 tablespoons vegetable oil
1/2 teaspoon salt

1. Preheat oven to 400°F.
2. Arrange tortilla quarters on cookie sheet and brush both sides with vegetable oil. Sprinkle with salt.
3. Bake for 8 to 10 minutes, or until crisp. Remove from oven and let cool to room temperature before eating.

Makes 6 servings.

Potato Crisps

2 large baking potatoes, scrubbed and cut into thin slices
2 tablespoons vegetable oil
1/2 teaspoon salt

1. Preheat oven to 375°F.
2. Arrange slices on a cookie sheet and brush both sides with vegetable oil. Sprinkle with 1/4 teaspoon salt.
3. Bake for 30 minutes or until golden brown and crispy. Remove from oven.

4. With a spatula, flip potatoes over and sprinkle with remaining salt.
5. Bake for another 15 to 20 minutes or until golden brown. Remove from oven and let cool to room temperature before eating.

Makes about 4 to 6 servings.

Seven-Layer Dip

1 16-ounce can refried beans
1 12-ounce jar salsa
8 ounces sour cream
2 cups iceberg lettuce, shredded
2 cups tomatoes, diced
2 cups cheddar cheese, shredded
1 6-ounce can pitted olives

In microwavable serving dish, layer beans, salsa, sour cream, lettuce, tomatoes, cheese, and olives. Microwave on high for 2 to 3 minutes, or until cheese is just melted. Serve immediately with chips.

Serves 6.

Party Popcorn

Toss one quart of popcorn with any of these fancy flavors:

CHEESY POPCORN

4 tablespoons grated sharp cheese
4 teaspoons melted butter
1/2 teaspoon garlic salt

CHOCOLATE POPCORN

1/4 cup sugar
1 1/2 teaspoons cocoa powder
1 1/2 teaspoons butter
2 tablespoons evaporated milk
1/8 teaspoon vanilla

Combine all ingredients in a saucepan and bring to a boil, stirring frequently. Pour over popcorn and toss.

MEXICAN POPCORN

2 tablespoons melted butter
1 tablespoon taco seasoning

TEX-MEX POPCORN

1 teaspoon chili powder
1 teaspoon paprika
1 teaspoon cumin
2 tablespoons melted butter

CINNAMON POPCORN

1 tablespoon sugar
1 1/2 teaspoons cinnamon
2 tablespoons melted butter

ZESTY POPCORN

4 tablespoons grated Parmesan cheese
1 tablespoon Italian seasoning
2 tablespoons melted butter

Dip-Stick Salad

FOR DIP:

   1/3 cup mayonnaise
   3/4 cup plain yogurt
   1 tablespoon fresh parsley, minced
   2 tablespoons ranch seasoning

1. Mix all ingredients thoroughly and chill.

Makes one cup (about 4 servings).

FOR STICK:

   plum tomatoes
   cheese, cut into 1/2-inch cubes
   bell peppers, cut into 1-inch squares
   broccoli florets
   cauliflower florets
   asparagus spears
   pitted olives

1. Spear various combinations of veggies and cheese on toothpicks or shish kebob skewers then dip and dine!

Crunchy Munchies

1/2 cup roasted cashews
1/2 cup almonds
1/2 cup yogurt-covered raisins
1/2 cup dried apricots
1/2 cup dried cranberries
1/2 cup dried mango slices
1/2 cup mini-chocolate chips
1/2 cup goldfish or mini-pretzels

1. Combine all ingredients and store in cool, dry place.

Makes 4 cups (8 to 12 servings).

Ants on Logs

2 celery stalks
3 tablespoons cream cheese
3 tablespoons peanut butter
2 tablespoons raisins

1. Slice each celery stalk into three "logs."
2. Fill three logs with peanut butter and three logs with cream cheese.
3. Press raisins along the tops of all the logs.

Makes 6 logs (2 servings).

227

Finger Knitting

*O*ne of the oldest forms of knitting, practiced by the people in ancient Egypt and Peru, is also one of the simplest. In the Northwest Territories of Canada, people who lived along the Mackenzie River would finger-knit long strands of snowshoe hare fur to make winter clothing. What'll it be for you? You can knit chokers, bracelets, or anklets. Try making a belt or a shoulder strap for a blue-jean pocket purse (see page 261). All you need is a ball of yarn and your fingers to get started. Happy knitting!

1. Let several inches of yarn dangle between your thumb and index finger on the back side of your hand. This will be the "tail" of your chain. Pass the ball of yarn around your thumb to make a loop.
2. Pass the yarn over the back of your index finger, under your middle finger, over your ring finger, and under your pinkie. Loop the yarn around your pinkie, then under your

ring finger, over your middle finger, and under your index finger. Be sure to keep the yarn just slightly loose.

3. Repeat step 2. Turn your palm toward you. Each finger should have two loops of yarn around it. Now you're ready to start knitting.

4. Lift the bottom loop on your pinkie over the top loop and off your finger. Repeat this for your ring, middle, and index fingers. Each finger should have the old top loop remaining. You've just knitted your first row.

5. To set up the second row, weave the yarn on the underside of your index finger, around the back of your middle finger, under your ring finger, around your pinkie, then back over your ring finger, under your middle finger, and over your index finger.

6. Lift all the bottom loops over the top loops and off your fingers as you did in step 4. Continue weaving the yarn in and out of your fingers and lifting off the bottom loops to make a new row.

7. When you're happy with the length of your chain, snip the strand of yarn several inches from the end of your chain. Carefully lift the remaining loops off your fingers and thread the end strand through each loop to keep it from unraveling.

There is a richness
in a life where
you stand on
your own feet. . . .
you set your own
ground rules, and
if you follow them,
there are great rewards.
—Margaret Bourke-White

Eleven-year-old Margaret has just moved from New York City to the New Jersey suburbs. Anxious to fit in at her new school, she joins a secret club—the Pre-Teen Sensations (PTS's)—in which she and her new girlfriends, Nancy, Gretchen, and Janie, discuss their developing bodies and boys. But Margaret needs someone with which to share her questions and fears. Despite not having been brought up according to an organized religion, she chooses to open her heart to God. Of Blume's more than two dozen books, *Are You There God? It's Me, Margaret* remains her most celebrated and controversial. Published in 1970, it opened doors in children's literature by offering an honest look at two topics that were off limits at the time. Being a target of censorship has led Blume to lend her voice to the cause of intellectual freedom.

Are you there God? It's me, Margaret. I'm in my new bedroom but I still have the same bed. It's so quiet here at night—nothing like the city. I see shadows on my wall and hear these funny creaking sounds. It's scary God! Even though my father says all houses make noises and the shadows are only trees. I hope he knows what he's talking about! I met a girl today. Her name's Nancy. She expected me to be very grown up. I think she was disappointed. Don't you think it's time for me to start growing God? If you could arrange it I'd be very glad. Thank you.

Are you there God? It's me, Margaret. I just told my mother I want a bra. Please help me grow God. You know where. I want to be like everyone else. You know God, my new friends all belong to the Y or the Jewish Community Center. Which way am I supposed to go? I don't know what you want me to do about that.

Are you there God? It's me, Margaret. I just did an exercise to help me grow. Have you thought about it God? About my growing, I mean. I've got a bra now. It would be nice if I had something to put in it. Of course, if you don't think I'm ready I'll understand. I'm having a test in school tomorrow. Please let me get a good grade on it God. I want you to be proud of me. Thank you.

Are You There God? It's Me Margaret

by Judy Blume

233

Are you there God? It's me, Margaret. I can't wait until two o'clock God. That's when our dance starts. Do you think I'll get Philip Leroy for a partner? It's not so much that I like him as a person God, but as a boy he's very handsome. And I'd love to dance with him . . . just once or twice. Thank you God.

Are you there God? It's me, Margaret. I hate to remind you God . . . I mean, I know you're busy. But it's already December and I'm not growing. At least I don't see any real difference. Isn't it time God? Don't you think I've waited patiently? Please help me.

Are you there God? It's me, Margaret. Life is getting worse every day. I'm going to be the only one who doesn't get it. I know it God. Just like I'm the only one without a religion. Why can't you help me? Haven't I always done what you wanted? Please . . . let me be like everybody else.

I locked the bathroom door and attached a Teenage Softie to the little hooks on my pink belt. Then I got dressed and looked at myself in the mirror. Would anyone know my secret? Would it show? Would Moose, for instance, know if I went back outside to talk to him? Would my father know it right away when he came home for dinner? I had to call Nancy and Gretchen and Janie right away. Poor Janie! She'd be the last of the PTS's to get it. And I'd been so sure it would be me! How about that! Now I am growing for sure. Now I am almost a woman!

Are you still there God? It's me, Margaret. I know you're there God. I know you wouldn't have missed this for anything! Thank you God. Thanks an awful lot. . . .

Questions

What is air?

Air is a gas that is primarily made of nitrogen and oxygen combined with small amounts of carbon dioxide, water, and other elements. Air is the substance that supports life on earth. While air is colorless, tasteless, and odorless, it does have weight and takes up space.

How do airplanes fly?

Airplanes are able to fly because of *lift*. Lift (the force that keeps airplanes in the air) is generated when air particles split at the edge of the wing, either going over or under the wing. The particles traveling over the top of the wing travel faster than those at the bottom. The air traveling under the plane pushes upward while the air traveling over the top pushes downward. This combined force lifts the plane's wings into the air.

What is lightning?

Lightning is electricity. Particles within a cloud become charged and separate into positive and negative regions. The upper portion of the cloud acquires a positive charge and the lower portion a negative one. This separation also creates electrical charges between the cloud and the ground. As the charges build and finally break down the surrounding air's electrical *resistance* (natural opposition to the flow of electricity), an electrical spark or flash occurs.

What is thunder?

Lightning actually causes thunder. Lightning heats the air at thousands of degrees in less than a second. When the air is heated this quickly, it expands and then contracts, creating sound waves.

What is a rainbow?

A rainbow is an optical effect that occurs when the sun's rays interact with rain droplets. The droplets act together, forming a prism (a transparent object or substance that refracts light), each droplet reflecting the white light of the sun off its inside surfaces, causing the light to bend. This bending makes the light's colors—red, orange, green, blue, indigo—visible.

Answers

In The Air

Because each color's wavelength bends a different amount, the colors separate into the spectrum. The order of the colors is always the same (red, orange, green, blue, indigo, and violet) unless there is a double rainbow, in which case the second rainbow's colors are reversed. A double rainbow occurs when light is reflected twice within a raindrop.

What is a cloud?

Clouds are dense clusters of ice crystals and/or rain droplets that form in the atmosphere. Clouds can take various shapes and sizes.

What is a silver lining in a cloud?

A silver "lining" appears in a cloud when light is *diffracted* (bent or spread out) by droplets along its edge. They most often appear along the edges of thicker clouds, which contain larger droplets. The saying "Every cloud has a silver lining" means that even though clouds are blocking the sun, the sun is still there ready to break out. Hence, behind every bad or difficult situation there's a brighter or better side.

What causes snowflakes?

When mist and water droplets within a cloud freeze (when the temperature is less than 32° F), they form ice crystals. When these crystals fall from the clouds, they join together, forming snowflakes. Every snowflake is a six-sided shape because of the way its water molecules bond. Each snowflake may contain as little as two or as many as two hundred individual crystals. The shape of a snowflake depends on the temperature outside. The colder the temperature, the smaller the snowflake; the warmer, the larger the flake. No two snowflakes are alike in appearance. *Interesting fact: Scientists have been able to create snowflakes in laboratories.*

237

Crying

by Galway Kinnell

Crying only a little bit
is no use. You must cry
until your pillow is soaked!
Then you can get up and **laugh**.
Then you can jump in the shower
and **splash-splash-splash!**
Then you can throw open your window
and, "Ha ha! ha ha!"
And if people say, "hey,
what's going on up there?"
"**Ha ha!**" sing back, "Happiness
was hiding in the last tear!
I wept it! **Ha ha!**"

When all the world is a hopeless jumble and
      the raindrops tumble all around,
Heaven opens a magic lane.
When all the clouds darken up the skyway,
      there's a rainbow highway to be found,
Leading from your window pane.
To a place behind the sun,
Just a step beyond the rain.

Somewhere over the rainbow way up high,
There's a land that I heard of once in a lullaby,
Somewhere over the rainbow skies are blue,
And the dreams that you dare to dream really do come true.

Someday I'll wish upon a star and wake up
      where the clouds are far behind me,
Where troubles melt like lemon drops, away above the chimney tops
      that's where you'll find me.
Somewhere over the rainbow bluebirds fly,
Birds fly over the rainbow, why then, oh why can't I?

If Happy little bluebirds fly beyond the rainbow, why, oh why, can't I?

Over the Rainbow

by E.Y. Harburg

Rainbow-a-Rama

*B*ecome an instant fashion designer and put a rainbow twist into your favorite clothes! You can personalize your old cotton T-shirts, pants, and socks with funky tie-dye patterns and colors. If that's not enough, you don't have to stop there—you can add a rainbow of color to sheets, pillowcases, and towels, too!

Fabric dye, rubber bands, coins or marbles, clothespins, rubber gloves, large bowls or buckets

1. Make sure the clothing you want to dye is clean and dry. Twist and tie various parts of the fabric with rubber bands. The tighter you secure the rubber bands, the crisper your patterns will be.

STARBURSTS Place a coin or marble underneath a layer of fabric where you'd like the center of the starburst to be and tie a rubber band tightly around it. Tie several more rubber bands underneath the first, spaced an inch or two apart, to add more rings to the starburst.

FUNKY STRIPES Gather the garment together lengthwise. Tie several rubber bands along the entire length of the clothing.

SPIRALS Pinch a segment of fabric with a clothespin and twist into a disc or cinnamon-roll shape. Secure the disc in place with a rubber band and leave the clothespin clamped on.

POLKA DOTS Place a marble or coin underneath the fabric and tie it in place with a rubber band. Add more coins and rubber bands to make as many dots as you like!

2. In a bowl or bucket, prepare the fabric dye in very hot water according to package instructions. Be sure to wear rubber gloves, or you might have green hands for a week!

3. Soak the rubber-banded clothes in the dye for at least 20 minutes. If you

want more than one color on the same garment, dip in lighter colors first, then the darker ones.

4. Remove the clothing from the dye solution and rinse in cold water until the water runs clear.

5. Remove all rubber bands, coins, marbles, or clothespins and . . . *Voilà!*

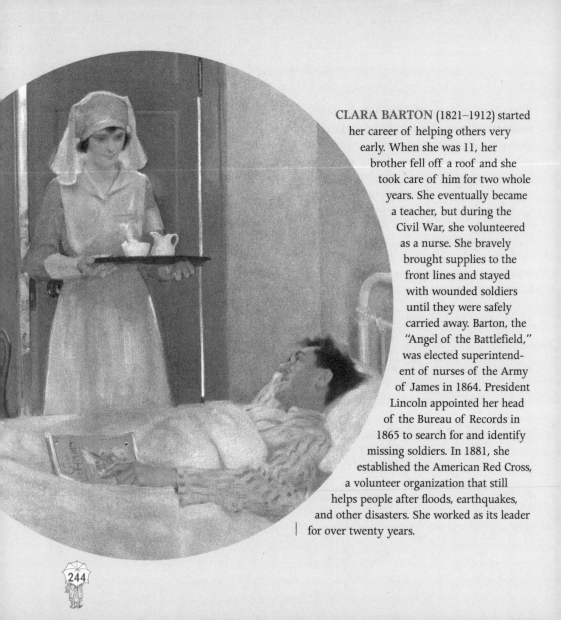

CLARA BARTON (1821–1912) started her career of helping others very early. When she was 11, her brother fell off a roof and she took care of him for two whole years. She eventually became a teacher, but during the Civil War, she volunteered as a nurse. She bravely brought supplies to the front lines and stayed with wounded soldiers until they were safely carried away. Barton, the "Angel of the Battlefield," was elected superintendent of nurses of the Army of James in 1864. President Lincoln appointed her head of the Bureau of Records in 1865 to search for and identify missing soldiers. In 1881, she established the American Red Cross, a volunteer organization that still helps people after floods, earthquakes, and other disasters. She worked as its leader for over twenty years.

HEROINES OF HEART

MARIE CURIE (1867–1934) was born into a family of teachers who did not have a lot of money but who prized knowledge over material possessions. A strong student, Curie got a physics degree even though she hadn't been able to afford a good education and had to teach herself much of the science. She went on to win the Nobel Prize for discovering two highly radioactive elements. Marie Curie's work was very important in developing X-rays, which allow doctors to see into the human body and treat problems.

MOTHER TERESA (1910–97) was only 12 when she knew that she wanted to help the poor. Born in Yugoslavia, she moved to India, but then went to Ireland at 18 to learn to become a nun. She returned to India and taught for twenty years at a high school in Calcutta. Beyond the windows, though, the poverty and suffering she saw made her want to help. In 1948, the Pope let her leave her school duties and take care of the poor and sick from the streets. Her efforts were so successful that she opened centers all around the world to help people. In 1979,

Mother Teresa's efforts were recognized with the Nobel Peace Prize.

FLORENCE NIGHTINGALE (1820–1910) came from a wealthy English family who expected her to marry well and become a wife and mother. She had other ideas. Nightingale wanted to help others, so she went to Germany and learned about medicine. In 1854, Britain, France, and Turkey declared war on Russia, and there were reports that the care for wounded soldiers was of very poor quality. Nightingale made her way to Turkey with thirty-eight nurses and greatly improved the situation. After the war, she returned to England and started a school just for nurses, who until then had not been well trained. For the first time in history, being a nurse became a respectable job for women, thanks to Nurse Nightingale.

If there is faith that can move mountains, it is faith in your own power.

—MARIE VON EBNER-ESCHENBACH

Rebecca Rowena Randall chatters as much as the brook that runs through her family's farm—a farm that she calls Sunnybrook. Now this talkative ten-year-old is on her way to Riverboro, Maine, to live with her aunts—stern Miranda and gentle Jane. Rebecca's widowed mother means to have her sisters teach her daughter how to be a proper lady. The years with her aunts prove difficult for irrepressible Rebecca with the mesmeric eyes. But her remarkable spirit wins even her "Aunt Mirandy" over in the end. Kate Douglas Wiggin (1856-1923) accomplished her first literary success with *The Bird's Christmas Carol* (1887). But it was with *Rebecca of Sunnybrook Farm* (1903) that the author made her mark. A sequel called *The New Chronicles of Rebecca* (1907) followed.

Rebecca sat down carefully, smoothing her dress under her with painstaking precision, and putting her sunshade under its extended folds between the driver and herself. This done she pushed back her hat, pulled up her darned white cotton gloves, and said delightedly:

"Oh! this is better! This is like traveling! I am a real passenger now, and down there I felt like our setting hen when we shut her up in a coop. I hope we have a long, long ways to go?"

"Oh! we've only just started on it," Mr. Cobb responded genially; "it's more 'n two hours."

"Only two hours," she sighed. "That will be half past one; mother will be at Cousin Ann's, the children at home will have had their dinner, and Hannah cleared all away. I have some lunch, because Mother said it would be a bad beginning to get to the brick house hungry and have Aunt Mirandy have to get me something to eat the first thing.—It's a good growing day, isn't it?"

"It is, certain; too hot, most. Why don't you put up your parasol?"

She extended her dress still farther over the article in question as she said, "Oh dear no! I never put it up when the sun

Rebecca of Sunnybrook Farm

by Kate Douglas Wiggin

249

shines; pink fades awfully, you know, and I only carry it to meetin' cloudy Sundays; sometimes the sun comes out all of a sudden, and I have a dreadful time covering it up; it's the dearest thing in life to me, but it's an awful care."

At this moment the thought gradually permeated Mr. Jeremiah Cobb's slow-moving mind that the bird perched by his side was a bird of very different feather from those to which he was accustomed in his daily drives. He put the whip back in its socket, took his foot from the dashboard, pushed his hat back, blew his quid of tobacco into the road, and having thus cleared his mental decks for action, he took his first good look at the passenger, a look which she met with a grave, childlike stare of friendly curiosity.

The buff calico was faded, but scrupulously clean, and starched within an inch of its life. From the little standing ruffle at the neck the child's slender throat rose very brown and thin, and the head looked small to bear the weight of dark hair that hung in a thick braid to her waist. She wore an odd little vizored cap of white leghorn, which may either have been the latest thing in children's hats, or some bit of ancient finery furbished up for the occasion. It was trimmed with a twist of buff ribbon and a cluster of black and

> At this moment the thought gradually permeated Mr. Jeremiah Cobb's slow-moving mind that the bird perched by his side was a bird of very different feather. . . .

orange porcupine quills, which hung or bristled stiffly over one ear, giving her the quaintest and most unusual appearance. Her face was without color and sharp in outline. As to features, she must have had the usual number, though Mr. Cobb's attention never proceeded so far as nose, forehead, or chin, being caught on the way and held fast by the eyes. Rebecca's eyes were like faith,—"the substance of things hoped for, the evidence of things not seen." Under her delicately etched brows they glowed like two stars, their dancing lights half hidden in lustrous darkness. Their glance was eager and full of interest, yet never satisfied; their steadfast gaze was brilliant and mysterious, and had the effect of looking directly through the obvious to something beyond, in the object, in the landscape, in you. They had never been accounted for, Rebecca's eyes. The schoolteacher and the minister at Temperance had tried and failed; the young artist who came for the summer to sketch the red barn, the ruined mill, and the bridge ended by giving up all these local beauties and devoting herself to the face of a child,—a small, plain face illuminated by a pair of eyes carrying such messages, such suggestions, such hints of sleeping power and insight, that one never tired of looking into their shining depths, nor of fancying that what one saw there was the reflection of one's own thought.

> It was trimmed with a twist of buff ribbon and a cluster of black and orange porcupine quills, giving her the quaintest and most unusual appearance.

Mr. Cobb made none of these generalizations; his remark to his wife that night was simply to the effect that whenever the child looked at him she knocked him galley-west.

"Miss Ross, a lady that paints, gave me the sunshade," said Rebecca, when she had exchanged looks with Mr. Cobb and learned his face by heart. "Did you notice the pinked double ruffle and the white tip and handle? They're ivory. The handle is scarred, you see. That's because Fanny sucked and chewed it in meeting when I wasn't looking. I've never felt the same to Fanny since."

"Is Fanny your sister?"

"She's one of them."

"How many are there of you?"

"Seven. There's verses written about seven children:—

Quick was the little Maid's reply,
O master! we are seven!

I learned it to speak in school, but the scholars were hateful and laughed. Hannah is the oldest, I come next, then John, then Jenny, then Mark, then Fanny, then Mira."

"Well, that IS a big family!"

"Far too big, everybody says," replied Rebecca with an unexpected and thoroughly grown-up candor that induced Mr. Cobb to murmur, "I swan!" and insert more tobacco in his left cheek.

"They're dear, but such a bother, and cost so much to feed, you see," she rip-

pled on. "Hannah and I haven't done anything but put babies to bed at night and take them up in the morning for years and years. But it's finished, that's one comfort, and we'll have a lovely time when we're all grown up and the mortgage is paid off."

"All finished? Oh, you mean you've come away?"

"Oh, you live on a farm, do ye? Where is it? —near to where you got on?"

"No, I mean they're all over and done with; our family 's finished. Mother says so, and she always keeps her promises. There hasn't been any since Mira, and she's three. She was born the day Father died. Aunt Miranda wanted Hannah to come to Riverboro instead of me, but Mother couldn't spare her; she takes hold of housework better than I do, Hannah does. I told Mother last night if there was likely to be any more children while I was away I'd have to be sent for, for when there's a baby it always takes Hannah and me both, for Mother has the cooking and the farm."

"Oh, you live on a farm, do ye? Where is it? —near to where you got on?"

"Near? Why, it must be thousands of miles! We came from Temperance in the cars. Then we drove a long ways to cousin Ann's and went to bed. Then we got up and drove ever so far to Maplewood, where the stage was. Our farm is away off from everywheres, but our school and meeting house is at Temperance, and that's only two miles. Sitting up here with you is most as good as climbing the meeting-house steeple. I know a boy who's been up on our steeple. He said the people and cows looked like flies. We haven't met any people yet, but I'm kind of disappointed in the cows;—they don't look so little as I hoped they would; still" (brightening) "they don't look quite as big as if we were down side of them, do they? Boys always do the nice splendid things, and girls can only do the nasty dull ones that get left over. They can't climb so high, or go so far, or stay out so late, or run so fast, or anything."

Mr. Cobb wiped his mouth on the back of his hand and gasped. He had a feeling that he was being hurried from peak to peak of a mountain range without time to take a good breath in between.

"I can't seem to locate your farm," he said, "though I've been to Temperance and used to live up that way. What's your folks' name?"

"Randall. My mother's name is Aurelia Randall; our names are Hannah Lucy Randall, Rebecca Rowena Randall, John Halifax Randall, Jenny Lind Randall, Marquis Randall, Fanny Ellsler Randall, and Miranda Randall. Mother named half of us and Father the other half, but we didn't come out even, so they both thought it would be nice to name Mira after aunt Miranda in Riverboro; they hoped it might do some good, but it didn't, and now we call her Mira. We are all named after somebody in particular. Hannah is Hannah at the Window Binding Shoes, and I am taken out of *Ivanhoe*; John Halifax was a gentleman in a book; Mark is after his uncle Marquis de

"We haven't met any people yet, but I'm kind of disappointed in the cows;— they don't look so little as I hoped they would."

255

Lafayette that died a twin. (Twins very often don't live to grow up, and triplets almost never—did you know that, Mr. Cobb?) We don't call him Marquis, only Mark. Jenny is named for a singer and Fanny for a beautiful dancer, but mother says they're both misfits, for Jenny can't carry a tune and Fanny's kind of stiff-legged. Mother would like to call them Jane and Frances and give up their middle names, but she says it wouldn't be fair to Father. She says we must always stand up for Father, because everything was against him, and he wouldn't have died if he hadn't had such bad luck. I think that's all there is to tell about us," she finished seriously.

"**"There wa'n't many names left when your mother got through choosin'!"**

"Land o' Liberty! I should think it was enough," ejaculated Mr. Cobb. "There wa'n't many names left when your mother got through choosin'! You've got a powerful good memory! I guess it ain't no trouble for you to learn your lessons, is it?"

"Not much; the trouble is to get the shoes to go and learn 'em. These are spandy new I've got on, and they have to last six months. Mother always says to save my shoes. There don't seem to be any way of saving shoes but taking 'em off and going barefoot; but I can't do that in Riverboro without shaming Aunt Mirandy. I'm going to school right along now when I'm living with Aunt Mirandy, and in two years I'm going to the seminary at Wareham; mother says it ought to be the making of me! I'm going to be a painter like Miss Ross when I get through school. At any rate, that's what I think I'm going to be. Mother thinks I'd better teach."

"Your farm ain't the old Hobbs place, is it?"

"No, it's just Randall's Farm. At least that's what Mother calls it. I call it Sunnybrook Farm."

"I guess it don't make no difference what you call it so long as you know where it is," remarked Mr. Cobb sententiously.

Rebecca turned the full light of her eyes upon him reproachfully, almost severely, as she answered:

"Oh! don't say that, and be like all the rest! It does make a difference what you call things. When I say Randall's Farm, do you see how it looks?"

"No, I can't say I do," responded Mr. Cobb uneasily.

"Now when I say Sunnybrook Farm, what does it make you think of?"

Mr. Cobb felt like a fish removed from his native element and left panting on the sand; there was no evading the awful responsibility of a reply, for Rebecca's eyes were searchlights that pierced the fiction of his brain and perceived the bald spot on the back of his head.

"I s'pose there's a brook somewheres near it," he said timorously.

Rebecca looked disappointed but not quite disheartened. "That's pretty good," she said encouragingly. "You're warm but not hot; there's a brook, but not a common brook. It has young trees and baby bushes on each side of it, and it's a shallow chattering little brook with a white sandy bottom and lots of little shiny pebbles. Whenever there's a bit of sunshine the brook catches it, and it's always full of sparkles the livelong day. Don't your stomach feel hollow? Mine does! I was so 'fraid I'd miss the stage I couldn't eat any breakfast."

Nobody has a better vision
of who you are than yourself.
—SHERYL CROW

Silk-Screen Prints

Silk-screening is one of the simplest forms of printing. It involves using a stencil that is applied to a fabric mesh stretched over a rigid frame. The secret to success is to plan ahead and work quickly before the paint starts to dry. You might want to practice on an old bed sheet or tablecloth first. Once you get a feel for the craft, you can decorate T-shirts and tote bags, or you can print on paper to make posters or greeting cards.

Cheesecloth, embroidery hoop, paper, pencil, vellum or other medium-weight semi-transparent paper, scissors, masking tape, fabric, fabric paint, Popsicle sticks.
Tip: This project can be messy, so you may want to keep a roll of paper towels handy

1. To make the silk screen, stretch several layers of cheesecloth in the hoop.
2. Create an image that you'd like to print. Draw your design on paper, making sure it will fit inside the screen.
3. Trace your pattern onto a sheet of vellum that is wider then the embroidery hoop. With scissors, carefully cut along the tracing lines to create a cut-out design in the vellum.
4. Trim the vellum so that it is slightly larger than the embroidery hoop. Place the vellum on top of the hoop. Make sure that the paper is flush with the screen, and tape the edges to the hoop.
5. Lay your fabric flat on a covered working surface. Place the silk screen (vellum side down) on top of the fabric where you want to print your design.
6. Pour a generous amount of fabric paint into the hoop just above your design. Use the Popsicle stick to spread the paint across the cheesecloth and over the vellum cutout.
7. Lift the silk screen off the fabric and place it on the next area to print. Smooth the paint over the surface of the cheesecloth again with the Popsicle stick.
8. Set aside the freshly printed fabrics until the paint has dried thoroughly.

Blue-Jean Bags

*T*he next time you want a beautiful bag, just turn your old hip-huggers into a new hip-slinger! You can recycle your favorite jeans into book bags or chic pocket purses decorated with buttons, beads, or appliqués. Now you'll be able to say that your old jeans will never die . . . they'll just go to waist!

Old blue jeans, scissors, tape measure, pins, needle, thread, fabric glue, ribbon, Velcro strips or snaps, appliqués (page 192) and other notions

Book Bag

1. Button up a pair of old jeans and turn them inside out. Have an adult help you cut off the pant legs about two or three inches below the crotch.
2. Line up the cut-off leg openings and pin them together. Sew them closed with a needle and thread, or glue them closed using fabric glue about an inch from the edge. Have an adult trim the edges about a half inch from the seam.
3. You can make a shoulder strap from one of the cut-off pant legs. Cut a strip of denim 25 inches long x 5 inches wide. Fold the fabric in half lengthwise with right sides facing each other. Sew or glue the long edges together about $1/4$ inch from the edge. Be sure to leave the ends open. Turn the strap right-side out.
4. Turn your bag right-side out. Pin the ends of your shoulder strap to the inside of the bag along the waist. Sew or glue the strap ends in place. Decorate.

Pocket Purse

1. Under adult supervision, remove a back pocket from an old pair of jeans by carefully cutting around the edge of the pocket. Be careful not to cut the seams (otherwise you'll only have half a pocket)!
2. Cut a length of ribbon for the shoulder strap. Pin the ribbon ends inside the pocket at each side. Sew or glue them in place.
3. With fabric glue or needle and thread, attach Velcro strips or snaps along the inside top of the pocket purse. Decorate.

More Twisters!

Tangle your tongue with these tongue tanglers!

If you notice this notice you will notice that this noti⸻

Lesser weather never weathered wetter weather better.

Six sick slick slim sycamore saplings.

A big black bug bit a big black bear, made the big bl⸻

not worth noticing.

Which witch wished which wicked wish?

There was a minimum of cinnamon in the aluminum pan.

two witches were watching two watches, which witch was watching which watch?

Cows graze in groves on grass. Which grows in grooves in groves.

bleed blood. Fred fed Ted bread, and Ted fed Fred bread.

Go Fish

A lazy day on the card pond

Number of players: three to five

Setup: Deal out seven cards to each player, and put the rest facedown in the "pool." Players remove any four-card sets from their hands. Players then organize their hands so that all cards with the same value (such as Jacks or 3s) are together.

Goal: To get the most four-card sets

How to play: First player asks one of the other players for a card that matches one she already has in her hand (only if she has one or more Jacks, for example, can she ask for

one). If the player she asks has the denomination—let's say Jacks—the player must give her all the Jacks she has. If the first player gets the card she wants, she asks for another card from the any player again. If the other player doesn't have the card the asker wants, the player tells the asker, "Go fish," from the pool. The asker takes one card from the pool. The player who said, "Go fish," becomes the next asker. Whenever a player collects all four of a kind, she puts the set faceup on the table. The game ends when one player is able to get rid of all her cards in matching sets.

War

An endless battle, but the winner takes all!

Number of players: two

Setup: Deal out the cards, half to yourself and half to the other player. Hold your cards facedown in a stack.

Goal: To get all the cards in the deck

How to play: You are the dealer. Your opponent places the top card from her stack faceup on the table, and you do the same.

Card
Games

Whoever played the higher card (the Ace is the highest, the 2 the lowest) takes both and adds them to the bottom of her stack. If both cards have the same value, it means "war." If the cards starting the war are both 2s, place two cards facedown and a third card faceup. Likewise, if the cards are 7s, place seven cards facedown, and so on (Jacks are worth 11 points, Queens 12, Kings 13, and Aces 1). If the deciding cards again match, the war continues in the same way. Whoever wins the war takes all the cards on the table. Continue in the same way as before, turning cards over, one pair at a time. When one player wipes the other out, the game is over!

Spoons

Watch out, or they'll be gone before you know it!

Number of players: three to thirteen

Supplies: spoons—one less than there are players

Setup: Dealer deals out four cards to each player and keeps the rest of the deck facedown. The spoons are piled in the middle of the circle of players.

Goal: To avoid getting stuck without a spoon

How to play: The idea is to collect four of a kind (9s of every suit, for example) as cards are passed around. Without looking at it, the dealer passes a card from the deck to the player on her right, who looks at it. She may pass it to the right or keep it and pass one of her own cards on. The dealer keeps passing cards to the right as fast as the players can take them. Each player may only have four cards in her hand at any time. The first player to get four of a kind quietly takes a spoon and waits for the other players to notice. In the grabbing frenzy that follows, someone always ends up without a spoon! The loser of each round gets a letter—first an *s*, then a *p*, and so on, until someone spells out the word *spoon*.

Variation: "Pig." Instead of playing with spoons, the first person to collect four of a kind puts her finger on her nose and waits for the others to notice and put their fingers on their noses. The last one to notice is the pig!

Gin Rummy

Pour yourself a glass of cool lemonade, and while away the hours on the porch.

Number of players: two

Setup: Deal out ten cards to yourself and ten cards to your opponent. Place the remaining cards facedown in a stack on the table. Remove the top card from the stack and place it faceup next to the pile: This is the discard pile.

Goal: To be the first to collect a full hand of three- and four-card sets

How to play: Players collect cards that go together either because they all have the same value (like the 8 of spades, the 8 of clubs, and the 8 of hearts) or are in order within the same suit (like the 10, Jack, Queen, and King of diamonds). If your opponent wants the first card in the deck, she puts it into her hand and discards one she doesn't want faceup on the discard pile. If she doesn't want the first card, you may take it. If neither of you wants it, your opponent draws a new card from the deck and discards one from her hand. You may then take what she discarded or draw a new card from the deck. The game is over when one player collects exactly two sets of three cards and one set of four cards. The winner shows that she's won by placing her last discarded card facedown on the discard pile.

Who are you?

by Emily Dickinson

I'm nobody! Who are you?
Are you nobody, too?
Then there's a pair of us – don't tell!
They'd banish us, you know.

How dreary to be somebody!
How public, like a frog
To tell your name the livelong day
To an admiring bog!

ARE YOU A GREEK GODDESS?

Once upon a time, Greek goddesses ruled atop Mount Olympus. Each had a particular domain and distinct personality. Which one are you most like?

Are you irresistible? Do you have a kind heart? Are you unpredictable? If so, then you are like…

Aphrodite. *It is said that the goddess of love and beauty sprang fully formed from the sea foam. In fact, her name means "foam-risen" in ancient Greek.*

Do you love animals? Are you independent? Do you enjoy spending your time in nature? Are you athletic? Is your temper short? If so, then you are like…

Artemis. *The goddess of the hunt and the moon is the patroness of unmarried women and youth, childbirth, and wild animals.*

Is your nickname "Miss Greenthumb"? Are you a loving soul? Do your moods change like the seasons? If so, then you are like…

Demeter. *The goddess of agriculture is the patroness of farmers.*

Do people tell you that you are as wise as an owl? Are you interested in crafts such as weaving? When conflict arises, are you able to stand strong? Are you slow to anger? If so, then you are like…

Athena. *The goddess of wisdom, handicrafts, and war is the patroness of Athens, and is often represented by an owl.*

Are you bold? Do you flaunt your accomplishments? Are you a jealous person? If so, then you are like…

Hera. *The queen of the Olympian deities is the protector of married women, childbirth, and the home. She is rarely seen without her pet peacock.*

Are you a homebody? Do you make a point of staying out of petty quarrels? Are you good-natured and loving? Is it important to you to make everyone around you feel valued? If so, then you are like…

Hestia. *The goddess of hearth and home is the protector of women, orphans, and lost children.*

Loops of Fun

String games have a long history among cultures throughout the world. The Navajos say that string games were a gift from Grandmother Spider. In Aborigine culture, adults and children share stories through string games. And many peoples in the South Pacific use string games as a way to keep their fingers agile, so that they will be good weavers and net makers. The string game described here is most commonly known as Jacob's Ladder, but is known throughout the world by many names, including The Fishnet, Calabash Net, and Osage Diamonds.

4–6 feet of butcher's string, nylon cord, or macramé cord

1. To make a loop, tie the string ends in a double knot.
2. Begin with your thumbs and pinkies on the inside of the loop. Stretch your hands apart until the string is taut.
3. Loop your right index finger underneath the string that runs across your left palm. Repeat with your left index finger. Pull your hands apart so the string is pulled tight.
4. Release your thumbs from their loops.
5. Reach your thumbs under all of the strings so they hook the farthest-away string, from the outside. Pull your thumbs back toward you (under all the other strings.)
6. Pass your thumbs over the near index-finger string, pick up the far index-finger string and return. You will now have two

loops on each thumb.

7. Release your pinkie fingers from their loops.
8. Stretch your pinkies over the string that is nearest to them and hook them under the next string.
9. Return your hands to the open position and release your thumbs from their loops.
10. Pass your thumbs over the index-finger loops and inside the pinkie-finger loops from below. Pick up the near pinkie string and return.
11. With your right thumb and index finger, grasp the near left index-finger string and move it over the left thumb. Your left index finger and thumb now share the same loop.
12. Repeat step 11 for your right hand.
13. There are now two loops around each thumb. Lift the bottom loop up and over the top loop and off the thumb.
14. Spread your fingers apart. Now, dip your index finger straight down into the tri-angular space formed between your thumb and index finger.
15. Release your pinkies from their loops as you carefully spread out your index fingers and thumbs and turn your palms away from you. You made Jacob's ladder!!

Step 8

Step 14

Step 15

TIP: Try to keep the string a little bit loose between your fingers as you work. This will allow you to move your fingers more easily. It also will allow the string to slide into position easily.

A Piece of Cake

These heavenly cakes don't have to bake in the oven, which makes them "cool" treats for spring and summer parties. For a super-quick Pink Lemonade Cake, you can easily substitute ready-made pound cake for yellow cake in the recipe. If you can't decide whether you prefer chocolate mousse to strawberry cream to mocha-toffee— don't! Make them all and have a party!

Strawberry Cream Dream

FOR CRUST:

> 1 1/2 cup chocolate wafer cookies,
> finely crushed
> 6 tablespoons butter, melted

Mix cookie crumbs and butter together. Press firmly into 9-inch pie plate. Freeze for one hour.

FOR FILLING:

> 1/2 cup boiling water
> 1 (7-gram) gelatin packet
> 8 ounces cream cheese, softened
> 2 teaspoons vanilla
> 1/2 cup sugar
> 1/2 cup sour cream
> 1 cup heavy (whipping) cream

1. Pour boiling water into a large glass measuring cup. Stir in gelatin until dissolved.
2. In a small bowl, whip cream cheese until soft. Add vanilla and sugar and beat until creamy. Add sour cream and beat well. Mix in dissolved gelatin until blended.
3. In a separate bowl, whip heavy cream until peaks start to form. Fold into cream-cheese mixture and pour into cookie crust.

FOR TOPPING:

> 4 cups strawberries, sliced
> 1/2 cup sugar
> 1 cup water
> 2 tablespoons cornstarch

1. Crush 1 cup of strawberries in a blender. In a saucepan, combine crushed strawberries, sugar, water, and cornstarch. Cook over medium heat and stir until thickened (2 to 5 minutes). Remove from heat.
2. Stir remaining strawberries into sauce. Refrigerate until well chilled.
3. Top cream cheese layer with strawberry mixture and serve.

Makes 8 to 10 servings.

Boysenberry Chocolate Mousse Cake

1¹/2 *cups chocolate wafer cookies, finely crushed*
6 *tablespoons butter, melted*
¹/2 *cup water*
6 *tablespoons sugar*
5 *egg yolks*
6 *ounces semisweet chocolate, melted*
3 *tablespoons boysenberry syrup*
3¹/2 *cups nondairy whipped topping*
whipped cream
fresh mixed berries

1. Mix cookie crumbs and butter until well blended. Press into a spring form pan along bottom and one inch up sides.
2. Stir water and sugar in a saucepan over medium-high heat. Bring to boil and cook for 1 minute. Remove from heat.
3. Gradually whisk egg yolks into sugar mixture until smooth. Continue to whisk over medium heat until mixture thickens. Remove from heat and pour into a large bowl.
4. Add chocolate and boysenberry syrup and whisk until blended. Fold in whipped topping. Pour filling into cookie crust.

Freeze until firm. Remove from spring form and let sit at room temperature for 15 to 20 minutes before slicing.
5. Garnish with whipped cream and fresh berries.

Makes 8 to 10 servings.

Pink Lemonade Cake

1 *quart vanilla ice cream or frozen yogurt, softened*
1 *(6-ounce) can frozen pink lemonade concentrate, thawed*
1 *box yellow cake mix*
16 *ounces heavy (whipping) cream*
2 *tablespoons sugar*
3 *drops red food coloring*

1. Line a 9-inch pie plate with wax paper. In large bowl, mix ice cream and three-fourths of the lemonade concentrate. Scoop mixture into lined pie plate and freeze for several hours until firm.
2. Prepare cake mix according to package directions. Pour batter into two 9-inch glass pie plates. Bake according to directions and cool.
3. Place one cake layer upside down on a serving plate. Arrange ice cream/lemonade

mixture as middle layer and top with second cake layer.

4. In a medium bowl, whip cream, sugar, remaining 1/4 can lemonade concentrate, and food coloring until stiff. Spread on top and sides of cake. Freeze for 1 hour before serving.

Makes 8 to 10 servings.

Mocha-Toffee Ice Cream Pie

For crust:

1 1/2 cup Oreo cookies, finely crushed
3 tablespoons butter, melted

Mix cookie crumbs and butter until well blended. Press crumbs firmly into 9-inch pie plate.

For filling:

2 cups coffee ice cream, softened
12 ounces caramel topping
2 cups chocolate ice cream, softened
2 cups nondairy whipped topping, thawed
1 English toffee bar, crumbled

1. Spoon coffee ice cream into crust and spread evenly. Freeze until firm, about 15 minutes.

2. Spread half of the caramel topping on top of the coffee ice cream.

3. Spread chocolate ice cream on top of the caramel layer. Freeze until firm, about 15 minutes.

4. Spread the remaining caramel topping on top of the pie. Arrange dollops of whipped topping in a circular pattern on top of the caramel layer and sprinkle with crumbled toffee bar. Freeze pie until firm, at least five hours.

5. Allow pie to stand at room temperature at least fifteen minutes before serving.

Makes 8 to 10 servings.

Gather out of star-dust
Earth-dust,
Cloud-dust,
Storm-dust,
And splinters of hail,
One handful of dream-dust
Not for sale.

Dream
Dust

by
Langston Hughes

Ebony & Ivory

by Paul McCartney

Ebony and Ivory live together in perfect harmony,
Side by side on my piano keyboard, oh Lord, why don't we?
We all know that people are the same wherever you go.
There is good and bad in ev'ryone, we learn to live
We learn to give each other what we need to survive
Together alive.

Ebony and Ivory live together in perfect harmony,
Side by side on my piano keyboard, oh Lord, why don't we?
Ebony, Ivory, living in perfect harmony,
Ebony, Ivory, ooh.
Side by side on my piano keyboard oh Lord, why don't we?

MUST-SEE MOVIES!

ALICE IN WONDERLAND (1985 TV) stars Steve Allen, Scott Baio, Natalie Gregory, Sid Caesar, Donna Mills. Made-for-TV movie that follows the classic tales of *Alice's Adventures in Wonderland* and *Through the Looking Glass*. A large cast of celebrities stars in this faithful adaptation.

ANNIE (1982) stars Albert Finney, Carol Burnett, Aileen Quinn. Broadway musical based on the "Little Orphan Annie" comic strip. The energetic redheaded girl finds adventure when she comes to live with stuffy tycoon Daddy Warbucks.

BRIGHT EYES (1934) stars Shirley Temple. Temple plays a young orphan caught up in a custody battle between crotchety Uncle Ned and a loving aviator. Shirley sings her famous song "On the Good Ship Lollipop."

BRINGING UP BABY (1938) stars Katharine Hepburn, Cary Grant. A screwball romantic comedy about a museum curator, a young woman, and a series of crazy adventures they have with Baby, a leopard.

E. T.: THE EXTRA TERRESTRIAL (1982) stars Henry Thomas, Drew Barrymore. A group of children must protect a space alien from being captured, and send him back to his home planet.

MUST-SEE MOVIES!

FREAKY FRIDAY (1976) stars Barbara Harris, Jodie Foster. A comedy about a mother and daughter who find their personalities switched and have to live each other's lives for one day.

THE JOURNEY OF NATTY GANN (1985) stars Meredith Salenger, John Cusack. A young tomboy courageously struggles to find her father during the Great Depression with the help of her wolf.

KIKI'S DELIVERY SERVICE (1989) voices of Kirsten Dunst, Phil Hartman, Matthew Lawrence. Animated feature about a young witch who starts an air courier service to help her fit into a new community.

LITTLE WOMEN (1933) stars Katharine Hepburn. The classic adaptation of Louisa May Alcott's novel about the four March girls and their adventures growing up.

THE MUPPETS TAKE MANHATTAN (1984) voices of Jim Henson, Frank Oz; stars Dabney Coleman, Joan Rivers. The Muppet crew travels to New York City to put on a musical, but runs into difficulties when Kermit loses his memory.

MY GIRL (1991) stars Anna Chlumsky, Macauley Culkin, Dan Ackroyd. Tagline: When your dad's an undertaker, your mom's in heaven, and your grandma's got a screw loose…it's good to have a friend who understands you. Even if he is a boy.

THE PRINCESS BRIDE (1987) stars Cary Elwes, Robin Wright, Billy Crystal. A funny fairy-tale story, with some quirky twists, about a beautiful princess and her brave hero, with some giants, miracle men, and an evil prince thrown in.

THE SECRET GARDEN (1993) stars Maggie Smith, Kate Maberly. Mary is a sour girl, raised in India, who moves to England. She unlocks the magic of a hidden garden and becomes part of a family in this touching movie.

SINGIN' IN THE RAIN (1952) stars Gene Kelly, Debbie Reynolds. One of the all-time best musicals about a silent movie studio in the 1920s switching to sound. Gene Kelly sings and dances incredibly in his role as a talented movie star.

THE SOUND OF MUSIC (1965) stars Julie Andrews. Rodgers and Hammerstein musical about a governess, Maria, sent to take care of the unruly von Trapp children. Maria teaches the children to sing ("My Favorite Things," "Do-Re-Mi") and wins a place in their hearts, as well as Captain von Trapp's.

THE WIZARD OF OZ (1939) stars Judy Garland. The classic story has Dorothy Gale on the road to Emerald City, looking for the Wizard of Oz in order to get back to her home in Kansas. Along the way, she meets the Scarecrow, the Lion, and the Tin Man, and battles the Wicked Witch of the West.

Additional favorites: *A Christmas Story; Anne of Green Gables; Back to the Future; Heidi; Pee-wee's Big Adventure; The 5,000 Fingers of Dr. T; Wallace & Gromit: The Wrong Trousers*

Young Velvet Brown lives, sleeps, and breathes horses. She can often be spotted around her village cantering, whinnying, and tapping her thigh with a switch. Her special keepsake box is always filled with paper horses she's cut and assembled from newspapers and magazines. Velvet frequently daydreams of jumping and grooming imaginary horses, and even prays for God to give her horses and to turn her into "the best rider in England." When Velvet wins an unruly mixed-breed horse at the fair raffle, she is overjoyed. Against all odds and the judgment of those around her, she is determined—with the help of Mi Taylor—to train her spirited steed Pie (for piebald) for the Grand National steeplechase. Like many children's classics, *National Velvet* (1935) was originally intended for adult readers. The most celebrated work of Enid Bagnold (1889-1981), the book was made into an award-winning film starring Elizabeth Taylor as Velvet and Mickey Rooney as Mi.

There were no more clear rounds till the piebald came, and when it came a murmur went up from the villagers who stood in the crowd.

"Jumping that animal!" said a voice.

"Why, that's the one she won at the raffle!"

The piebald strode flashing into the sun. He paused, stood still, and gazed round him. Velvet's knees held him steadily, and she sat behind his raised neck without urging him on.

"I don't expect anything . . ." she whispered. "Do what you can. Keep steady. You're all right."

"You next," said a man at the bar of the Collecting Ring. "You waiting for anything?"

"I'm going," said Velvet quietly. "He just wants to look round."

Mi saw them come down the grass, the piebald trotting with a sort of hesitation.

"He's in two minds whether he'll bolt," thought Mi.

"Showy horse . . ." said a spectator.

"Butcher's girl . . ." said another. "The youngest. Got a seat, 'ant she?"

The piebald's eye was towards the crowd, his white eye to the center of the field.

The trot broke hesitatingly into a canter, but the horse had no concentration in him. He looked childishly from side to side, hardly glancing at the jump ahead.

National Velvet

by Enid Bagnold

"He'll refuse," said Mally, who had arrived at Mi's side. But Mi made no answer.

Sir Pericles had jumped like a trained horse. The piebald's jumping was a joke. Arrived at the jump in another two paces, he appeared to be astonished, planted his forelegs for a second, looked down, trembled, then leaped the little bush and rail with all four legs stiff in the air together. Dropping his hindquarters badly he came down on the rail and broke it in two.

"Two faults," said Mi.

"Only two for breaking that?"

Hind feet. Only two."

> Dropping his hind-quarters badly he came down on the rail and broke it in two. "Two faults," said Mi.

Again the piebald trotted, flashing, his grass-fed belly rounded, and his shoulders working under the peculiar color of his hide.

"Why don't she canter 'im?" said a voice.

Mi turned on the voice. "First time he's seen anything but his own grazing. It's a miracle if she gets him round."

"The In-and-Out'll finish him," said Mally under her breath.

The piebald jumped willingly into the In-and-Out, then paused, and remained inside.

A shout of laughter went up from the crowd.

"Oh . . . poor Velvet . . ." murmured Malvolia, agonized.

The piebald attempted to graze, as though he were in a sheep pen, and again the crowd laughed.

"She's handling him gentle," said Mi. "She's trying to keep him thinking he's a winner. She's backin' him, see. . . . I don't believe he's ever backed a pace before." The piebald had backed two paces till his quarters lay against the first jump of the In-and-Out. With a light heart he responded to his rider, and with a spring he was out again and cantering on.

"Do they count that as a fault?"

"I don't know," said Mi. "Watch out . . . now. . . . It's the Gate."

The piebald broke the gate. He would have liked a stout, stone wall, but this flimsy thing that stood up before him puzzled him and he did his goat-jump. All four legs in the air at once and landed back upon the laths and broke them.

"That horse is breaking up the field," said a voice.

Mi glared. "He's knocked his hock," said Mi; "that'll learn him." For the piebald limped a pace or two. It "learned" him. Unlettered as he was he had no thought of refusing. He saw the friendly wall ahead, and taking it to be enduring flint he went for it with a glare of interest, ears pricked and eyes bright. The wall was three foot six. He leaped five. For a second it seemed to the crowd as though the horse had nothing to do with the wall but was away up in the air. A little cheer went up and hands clapped in a burst.

"Don't she ride him!" said the voice. "It's that Velvet girl. The ugly one."

"What, that kid with the teeth?"

"That's who it is."

Mi knew that Mally's beauty stood beside him and he resented it. He half turned his shoulder on her. While Velvet sat the piebald he thought her the loveliest thing on earth. Like Dan, his father, he hardly saw the faces of women.

"Hullo, she's missed the stile!"

"Did he refuse?" asked Mi, keenly.

"I don't think she saw it," said Mally. "She simply rode on."

The judge waved his stick and called to a Starter. Velvet cantered, glowing, radiant, to the exit gate. The man who held the exit spoke to her and pointed. Velvet looked behind her, paused, then shook her head.

"Not coming . . ." shouted the man to the Steward.

After a brief pause . . .

"The last Competitor," announced the Broadcaster, "did not complete the round."

"Why ever didn't she!" said Mally, as she and Mi left the rope to fight their way round to the tree. They scrambled out from the crowd and ran.

Velvet was standing looking at the piebald as though bemused. Merry, her face happy with pride, was holding the horses.

"Marvelous, Velvet, to get him round!" said Mally, coming up. "Why didn't you jump the last jump?"

Velvet turned and looked, and Mi could see how her face was shining.

"I thought I'd better not," she said gently.

"Why?"

"He did the wall so beautifully I thought he'd better end on that."

There will always be dreams grander or humbler than your own, but there will never be a dream exactly like your own... for you are unique and more wondrous than you know!

—Linda Staten

Dreams,

Dreams,

Dreams...

The future belongs to those who believe in the beauty of their dreams. —Eleanor Roosevelt

Only as high as I reach can I grow,
Only as far as I seek can I go,
Only as deep as I look can I see,
Only as much as I dream can I be.

—Karen Ravn

The Circle Game

by Joni Mitchell

And the seasons they go round
and round, And the painted
ponies go up and down. We're
captive on the carousel of time.
We can't return we can only
look behind from where we came.
And go round and round and round
In the circle game.

294

Yesterday a child came out to wonder
Caught a dragonfly inside a jar
Fearful when the sky was full of thunder
    And tearful at the falling of a star

    (Chorus)

    Then the child moved ten times round the seasons
      Skated over ten clear frozen streams
      Words like, when you're older, must appease him
      And promises of someday make his dreams

    (Chorus)

    Sixteen springs and sixteen summers gone now
    Cartwheels turn to car wheels through the town
    And they tell him,
    Take your time, it won't be long now
    Till you drag your feet to slow the circles down

    (Chorus)

  So the years spin by and now the boy is twenty
 Though his dreams have lost some grandeur coming true
There'll be new dreams, maybe better dreams and plenty
Before the last revolving year is through.

Little Abigail and the Beautiful Pony

by Shel Silverstein

THE PONY THAT THEY WOULDN'T BUY ME. TOO LATE!

There was a girl named Abigail
Who was taking a drive
Through the country
With her parents
When she spied a beautiful sad-eyed
Grey and white pony.
And next to it was a sign
That said,
FOR SALE—CHEAP.
"Oh," said Abigail,
"May I have that pony?
May I please?"
And her parents said,
"No you may not."
And Abigail said,
"But I MUST have that pony."
And her parents said,
"Well, you can't have that pony,
But you can have a nice butter pecan
Ice cream cone when we get home."

And Abigail said,
"I don't want a butter pecan
Ice cream cone,
I WANT THAT PONY—
I MUST HAVE THAT PONY."
And her parents said,
"Be quiet and stop nagging—
You're *not* getting that pony."
And Abigail began to cry and said,
"If I don't get that pony I'll die."
And her parents said, "You won't die.
No child ever died yet from not getting a pony."
And Abigail felt so bad
That when they got home she went to bed,
And she couldn't eat,
And she couldn't sleep,
And her heart was broken,
And she DID die—
All because of a pony
That her parents wouldn't buy.

(This is a good story
To read to your folks
When they won't buy
You something you want.)

OH, IF, SHE WERE ONLY ALIVE I WOULD BUY HER A HUNDRED A HUNDRED PONIES!

OH... WHAT FOOLS WE WERE

TAKING CARE OF PETS

DOGS: Of all the common family pets, dogs definitely need the most care. First of all, they need to be exercised regularly. They love a brisk walk around your neighborhood, but don't forget to scoop the poop they leave behind! Dogs need as much love and attention as you can give them and they will return it in abundance.

CATS: While cats are more independent than dogs, they still need plenty of care and attention. Sometimes their mischief is simply a way of saying, "Pay attention to me, NOW!" If your cat lives indoors, you will have to keep her litter box as clean as she would keep it, if only she had thumbs!

BIRDS: The most important thing about taking care of your bird is a good cage. Different birds have different needs: Some love to fly short distances, some love to climb. The cage should be big enough to keep your bird happy and well exercised and safe enough that she won't escape or get stuck between the bars. Birds love toys and mirrors: Gazing at their reflections keeps them quite entertained!

RODENTS: Of all pets, rodents require the least amount of care. Some rodents, like hamsters and guinea pigs, love to play with humans, while others, like mice, are happy to spend all their time in their cage. Either

PET POPULARITY!

The most popular pets in the United States:

1 CATS—there are more than 66 million of them!

2 DOGS—there are 58 million of them, including 158 breeds of dogs and mutts.

3 BIRDS, more than 32 million feathered friends, including parakeets, finches, cockatiels, canaries, and parrots.

4 SMALL MAMMALS—more than 14 million—including rabbits, guinea pigs, gerbils, hamsters, and ferrets.

5 FRESHWATER FISH—more than 10 million homes have fish living in them.

6 REPTILES—7.5 million—including frogs, lizards, turtles, tortoises, and snakes.

way, all rodents need a secure cage that's big enough for all the exercise they need. Their cages should be stocked with a floor covering of wood shavings (not cedar) and soft bedding (bathroom tissue works fine), as well as rodent food and fresh water in a bottle. They also should have plenty of things to chew on—rodents have teeth that never stop growing, and constant gnawing helps keep the teeth in check.

REPTILES: Reptiles eat all sorts of things—some eat only plants and fruit, some eat only insects, some only other animals, and some like to pick and choose among those categories. The most important thing is that you understand which diet is right for your pet. The same goes for environment: Reptiles are all cold-blooded, which means they must get warmth from their surroundings. Different species need different levels of warmth and humidity.

FISH: Keeping fish, especially tropical fish, can be quite tricky. Even with a goldfish, the proper amount of food is essential for a happy and long-living fish. Also essential is keeping the tank cleaned and maintained, which can be quite expensive.

POPULAR PUPS AND THEIR PERSONALITIES

The 10 most popular dog breeds in the U.S. are:

LABRADOR RETRIEVER Whether yellow, black, or chocolate, the Lab is America's favorite dog. Playful, friendly, and reliable, Labs make the perfect family pet.

GOLDEN RETRIEVER Golden retrievers are big, sturdy dogs that love to please. Outgoing, devoted, happy, and trusting, they have all the qualities you'd expect of a great friend.

GERMAN SHEPHERD Brave, easy to train, intelligent, and always watchful, it's no wonder that German shepherds have so many jobs: police dogs, guide dogs, search-and-rescue dogs, bomb detectors, livestock herders, and of course, family pets!

DACHSHUND Who doesn't find the long body, short little legs, and wacky personality of the dachshund adorable? Their name means "badger dog" in German, as they were bred to burrow into small places to hunt badgers.

BEAGLE Beagles belong to a breed of hunting dogs that in real life hate to be alone. Beagles are happy, strong, and willful, and are always looking for the adventures that lie beyond the backyard.

YORKSHIRE TERRIER Though tiny, yorkies are terriers from teeth to tail—they love to play and investigate, and still have the hunting instinct bred into all terriers. Their long coat may be beautiful, but it means a lot of grooming work.

POODLE The three sizes of poodle, from largest to smallest, are standard, miniature, and toy. They are exactly the same in every way but size. Throughout history poodles have been used as truffle hunters, have aided game hunters as water retrievers, and have performed in circuses!

BOXER Extremely energetic, big, and playful, boxers wear their emotions on their faces. They are boisterous but also responsible—they often serve as police and military dogs.

CHIHUAHUA This is the smallest breed of dog. They can live to be 18 years old (much longer than bigger dogs) and spend those years as bouncing bundles of energy—Chihuahuas are quick, graceful, and always excited to see you.

SHIH TZU Little, proud, happy, and beautiful, this dog was bred as the perfect house pet and companion. The long, thick, and dense coat needs constant grooming—the prize—a magnificently fancy pet!

PET NAMES

According to the American Society for the Prevention of Cruelty to Animals (ASPCA), the twenty-one most popular pet names in America are:

1. Max	8. Molly	15. Pepper
2. Sam	9. Buddy	16. Jake
3. Lady	10. Brandy	17. Bandit
4. Bear	11. Ginger	18. Tiger
5. Smokey	12. Baby	19. Samantha
6. Shadow	13. Misty	20. Lucky
7. Kitty	14. Missy	21. Muffin

Pets

by
Margaret J. Miller

We had a cat, but that is gone---
'Twas always getting trodden on;
It ate (this was its favorite vice)
All it could get (excepting mice).
And nightly it would prowl and roam
And make a most terrific row;
We had to give it to a Home:
We only keep a goldfish now.

We had a dog -- a charming pup --
He liked to sleep upon my bed;
He rooted all the roses up
And planted all his bones instead.
The toughest tramp that begs at doors
To pat his back he would allow,
And yet he bit our visitors:
We only keep a goldfish now.

We once had hens -- they wouldn't lay,
Although for hours they sat and sat;
Our tame canary, sad to say,
Was eaten by the neighbor's cat.
Mice, rabbits, squirrels, birds, we've had --
Quite everything (except a cow):
But disillusioned, wise, and sad,
We only keep a goldfish now.

CLAP YOUR HANDS!

There are hundreds of wonderful clapping games that are fun to learn – you can even make up your own. No equipment required! All you need is a friend who knows the rhymes and moves or is willing to learn them. You can also play clapping games in larger groups by standing in a circle. Each rhyme has its own variations, where you can pat your shoulders, hands or thighs and clap hands with your partner! One or two hands at a time, backs of hands, palms, double claps, hands up, hands down! Play and play, clap and clap, beginning slowly and speeding up to get faster both in the chants and claps! Have fun creating clapping patterns to go along with these rhymes:

MISS MARY MACK

Miss Mary Mack, Mack, Mack,
All dressed in black, black, black,
With silver buttons, buttons, buttons,
All down her back, back, back
She asked her mother, mother, mother,
For fifty cents, cents, cents,
To see the elephant, elephant, elephant
Jump over the fence, fence, fence.
He jumped so high, high, high,
He reached the sky, sky, sky,
And he never came back, back, back,
'Till the end of July, 'ly, 'ly.

OH LITTLE PLAYMATE!

Oh little Playmate
Come out and play with me
And bring your dollies three,
Climb up my apple tree,
Holler down my rain barrel
Slide down my cellar door
And we'll be jolly friends forever more.

No, no, no playmate, I cannot
    play with you
My dollies have the flu,
Boo hoo hoo hoo hoo hoo,
Ain't got no rain barrel,
Ain't got no cellar door,
But we'll be jolly friends forever more.

MISS LUCY

Miss Lucy had a baby
His name was Tiny Tim
She put him in the bathtub
To see if he could swim
He drank up all the water
He ate up all the soap
He tried to eat the bathtub
But it wouldn't go down his throat
Miss Lucy called the doctor
Miss Lucy called the nurse
Miss Lucy called the lady
With the alligator purse
Measles said the doctor
Mumps said the nurse
Nothing said the lady
With the alligator purse
Miss Lucy kicked the doctor
Miss Lucy punched the nurse
Miss Lucy paid the lady
With the alligator purse

Fun Frozen Fruits

Satisfy your sweet tooth with these delectable treats. Real fruit is the secret ingredient that makes the taste of the tropics pop in your mouth. Frozen Blackberry Dream looks as delicious as it tastes in fancy Chocolate Bowls. You can make the bowls anytime and fill them with fresh fruits, yogurts, ice cream, or mousse for a quick and tasty dessert.

Blackberry Dream in Chocolate Bowls

FOR CHOCOLATE BOWLS:

>   12 ounces semisweet chocolate chips or
>   baking squares
>   12 foil baking cups

1. In a microwavable bowl, microwave chocolate on high in 1-minute intervals until melted, stirring in between timings.
2. Drop a couple of teaspoons of melted chocolate into each baking cup. Use the back of the spoon or a spatula to coat the bottom and sides of each cup. Freeze for 15 minutes or until chocolate has hardened.
3. Coat each baking cup with another layer of chocolate and return to freezer.

FOR FRUIT FILLING:

>   1 packet (1 1/2 teaspoons) unflavored gelatin
>   1/4 cup blackberry juice
>   3 cups blackberries
>   2 tablespoons sugar
>   1 tablespoon lemon juice
>   2/3 cup vanilla yogurt

1. In a glass measuring cup, soften gelatin in blackberry juice. Set measuring cup in a pan of hot water and stir until gelatin dissolves thoroughly.
2. In blender, combine blackberries, sugar, and lemon juice and mix for one minute. Strain into a medium-size bowl.
3. Add gelatin mixture and yogurt to pureed blackberries. Whisk until blended. Freeze for 1 to 2 hours.
4. In blender, mix chilled blackberry mixture for one minute until smooth. Pour mixture into chocolate cups and freeze 4 to 5 hours before serving.   *Makes 12 servings.*

Island Pops

>   1 3-ounce package strawberry gelatin
>   1/2 cup boiling water
>   1 tablespoon lemon juice
>   1 20-ounce can pineapple chunks, in juice
>   1 banana, sliced
>   6–8 strawberries, sliced
>   8 6-ounce paper cups
>   8 Popsicle sticks

1. In a glass measuring cup, mix gelatin with boiling water until dissolved.
2. Pour mixture into a blender. Add lemon juice, pineapple chunks with juice, banana, and strawberries. Puree until liquefied.
3. Pour mixture evenly into eight paper cups. Cover each cup with aluminum foil and insert a Popsicle stick into the center of each cup. Freeze overnight.   *Makes 8 pops.*

Glass Lake Figure Skater

What if you could skate like Olympic champions Michelle Kwan and Sarah Hughes? Even if you don't have a pair of ice skates, you can make your own magnetic skaters on a "frozen lake" that's perfect for figure eights, Axel spins, and graceful glides. With a few extra magnets, you can stage a world-class event, complete with colorful costumes for each contestant. Who'll win the gold? You be the judge!

White construction paper, scissors, glue, colored markers, gold or silver glitter, small round magnet, shoebox with lid, aluminum foil, tape, rhinestones (optional), bar magnet

1. To make your figure skater, start with a piece of construction paper about 8 inches long and 2 inches wide. Fold it in half crosswise. Then fold each loose edge back 1 inch, make a crease, and straighten out the flaps. Glue all but the flaps together. Let dry.
2. Draw your figure skater on the construction paper. The bottom of her skates should touch the crease of the 1-inch flaps. Give your skater a beautiful hairdo and a gorgeous outfit. You can add a thin layer of glue to her hair, dress, and skates, sprinkle on glitter, shake off excess, and let dry.
3. Cut out your skater, leaving the bottom flaps attached to the figure. Fold each flap out. Your skater should now be "standing" on a base. Center and glue the small round magnet to the bottom of the base. Trim away excess flaps.
4. To make the ice rink, wrap shoebox lid and shoebox separately with foil (try to keep foil smooth). Secure edges with tape. To decorate, glue rhinestones along edges of lid.
5. Make your skater glide across the ice by placing her on top of the shoebox lid and holding the bar magnet underneath lid. Now watch your main attraction twirl and dance on ice. Store your treasures in your new fun and sparkling box!

TENNIS

Known for her poise on the court, **CHRIS EVERT** (b.1954), won at least one Grand Slam title every year from 1974 to 1986. That includes six U.S. Open titles and three Wimbledon titles.

ALTHEA GIBSON (b.1927) was the New York State black girls' singles champion at fifteen, and in 1957 and 1958, went on to become the women's singles champion at Wimbledon and at the U.S. women's clay court championship, and won the U.S. Open.

BILLIE-JEAN KING (b.1943) started playing tennis at 11, and went on to win a record twenty Wimbledon titles. In a famous battle of the sexes, this outspoken woman defeated Bobby Riggs in 1973.

MARTINA NAVRATILOVA (b.1956) was a tennis star in the then Soviet Union before she defected to America in 1975. She won the women's singles at Wimbledon a record nine times, won four U.S. Open titles, and became the all-time leader, man or woman, in singles titles.

VENUS WILLIAMS (b.1980) has captured the attention of the world with her youth, style, and amazing sports abilities. Her serve (127 mph) is the fastest in women's professional tennis history. To date, she's won two Wimbledon titles and two U.S. Open titles.

SERENA WILLIAMS (b.1981), the very talented sister of Venus Williams, in 1999 became the first African-American woman to win a U.S. Open title since Althea Gibson in 1958.

311

GYMNASTICS

NADIA COMANECI (b.1961) was only 6 when she was noticed by famed coach Bela Karolyi. With his help, she won six medals (three gold, one silver, and one bronze) for her home country, Romania, in the 1976 Olympics.

OLGA KORBUT (b.1956) attended a special government-sponsored school in the Soviet Union when she was 11 and learned enough to eventually win two silver and four gold medals. Later, she moved to the United States and became a gymnastics instructor.

MARY LOU RETTON (b.1968) became the first American woman ever to win the gold medal in the All-Around in women's gymnastics, at the 1984 Olympics. She won more medals than any other athlete that year. Her smile also earned her a place on the front of the Wheaties cereal box.

FIGURE SKATING

PEGGY FLEMING (b.1948) took ballet classes as a child and used many of those graceful moves when she took up skating at the age of 9. In 1968, she won the gold medal in women's figure skating at the winter Olympics in France.

In the 1970s, DOROTHY HAMILL (b.1956) was one of America's most popular celebrities. After winning five consecutive world professional titles, three national titles, and one Olympic gold medal, she went on to actually buy the Ice Capades tour and be its artistic director.

MICHELLE KWAN (b.1980) first wanted to skate at the age of 6, when she saw her brother play hockey. She studied for years and went on to win four world titles, a silver Olympic medal, and many admirers with her artistic performances.

The popular KATARINA WITT (b.1965) was only 5 when she started figure skating. She eventually won two Olympic gold medals for her home country of Germany.

At 14 years old, TARA LIPINSKI (b. 1982) was already the youngest skater to win the U.S. National Champion title when she skated to gold in 1997. But when she was 15 years old, she also became the youngest Olympic champion on ice at the 1998 Games in Nagano.

TRACK & FIELD

JACKIE JOYNER-KERSEE (b.1962) went to college on a basketball scholarship, but she has many more talents. In fact, when she competed in the Olympic contest called the heptathlon, she did so well at running, high-jumping, shot putting, and javelin throwing, that she won the gold medal and set the world, Olympic, and American records in the event. Some consider this African-American heroine the world's best all-around female athlete.

Jackie Joyner-Kersee's sister-in-law, FLORENCE GRIFFITH JOYNER (1959–98), was a great athlete in her own right. She started running track when she was only 7, and grew up to win gold medals in the 100- and 200-meter races and in the 400-meter relay at the 1988 Olympic Games in Seoul, Korea.

When WILMA RUDOLPH (1940–94) was 4 years old, she had polio. She couldn't walk without leg braces until the age of 9. Because she was African-American, she had to travel far away to get care at a black medical college. She grew stronger, though, and even became a basketball star in high school. Then, when she was only 16, she went to the 1956 Olympics in Melbourne, Australia, and won a bronze medal in the 4 x 4 relay. Four years later, in Rome, she ran so fast that she became the first American woman to win three gold medals in the Olympics. Wilma is one of the most celebrated female athletes in history.

SOCCER

MIA HAMM (b. 1972), perhaps the most recognized female soccer player in the world, broke the international scoring record for men and women on May 16, 1999, with her 108th career goal in a game against Brazil. Heavily marked on the field, she regularly has two or three opposing defenders placed on her whenever she has possession of the ball.

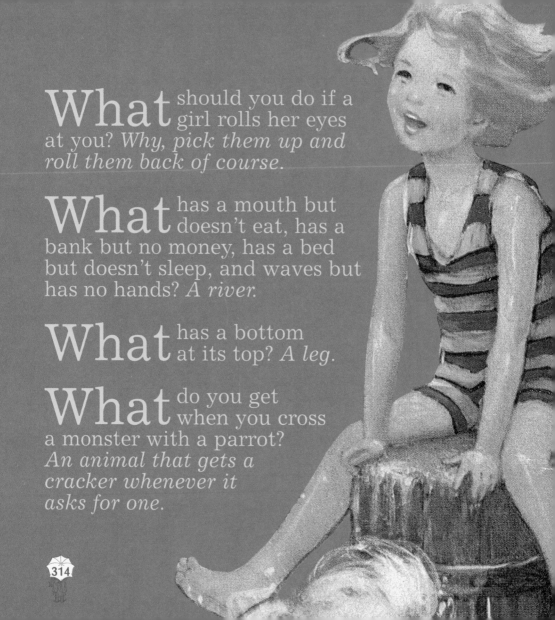

What should you do if a girl rolls her eyes at you? *Why, pick them up and roll them back of course.*

What has a mouth but doesn't eat, has a bank but no money, has a bed but doesn't sleep, and waves but has no hands? *A river.*

What has a bottom at its top? *A leg.*

What do you get when you cross a monster with a parrot? *An animal that gets a cracker whenever it asks for one.*

THAT'S FUNNY!

What is white when it's dirty and black when it's clean? *A chalkboard.*

How do you make a venetian blind? *Stick your finger in his eye!*

Why are pianos hard to open? *Because all the keys are inside.*

What do giraffes have that no other animal has? *Baby giraffes.*

Why do birds fly south in the winter? *Because it's too far to walk.*

What happened to the cat who swallowed a ball of wool? *In two months she had mittens.*

HOMONYMS

Are you a jokester? Do you love puns—that is, plays on words with the same or similar sounds? Then you are probably already a fan of the homonym, a word that has multiple meanings. Here is a joke that makes use of homonyms: What do you get when you feed a cat a lemon? A sour puss. The punch line contains two homonyms. "Sour," which can mean "tart" or "bad-tempered," and "puss," which can mean "cat" or "face." See if you can discover the double meanings of the homonyms (in bold) in the following jokes:

Why don't witches wear flat hats?

There's no **POINT**!

How did the telephone propose to the cell phone?

He gave her a **RING**!

Why was the bride sad at her wedding?

Because she couldn't marry the **BEST MAN**!

How many **FEET** are in a **YARD**?

It depends on how many people
show up at your picnic.

HOMOPHONES

As anyone trying to master English as a second language can tell you, homophones—words that sound alike but have different meanings—are slippery business. In fact, they can be difficult even for native speakers. Here are a few common examples: brake and break; hoarse and horse; knight and night; moose and mousse; plain and plane; sea and see. See if you can fill in the blanks of these sentences that use homophones:

It didn't make any _____ to Chloe when the shopkeeper gave her ten _____ change for her pack of chewing gum that she thought cost a dollar.

"How could it _____?" asked Billy. "Gretchen is such a poor speller, yet she won the spelling _____?"

Stuck in a daydream, Amelia wondered _____ whether or not she would be _____ to go to the dance on Saturday with Alex.

The show horse had been trotting but changed its _____ just before jumping over the _____ .

(*Answers: sense, cents; be, bee; aloud, allowed; gait, gate)*

Word Fun!

"Oh, I would love to take out the garbage," Susie said sweetly, "But there's the **automysophobia**—my fear of getting dirty," "And I would love to mend that dress I ruined last week, but Mommy! my **belonephobia**—those pins really make me squeak!" "Mmmmm..then," said Mommy, thoughtful and composed, "with my **ailurophobia** and **chrometophobia**, we can't get your new cat I suppose."

IFEARAPHOBIA

ACHLUOPHOBIA
Fear of darkness

ACOUSTICOPHOBIA
Fear of noise

ACROPHOBIA
Fear of heights

AGLIOPHOBIA
Fear of pain

AICHMOPHOBIA
Fear of pointed objects

AILUROPHOBIA
Fear of cats

ALLIUMPHOBIA
Fear of garlic

APIPHOBIA
Fear of bees

ARACHNOPHOBIA
Fear of spiders

AUTOMYSOPHOBIA
Fear of being dirty

BELONEPHOBIA
Fear of pins and needles

BLENNOPHOBIA
Fear of slime

CATOPTROPHOBIA
Fear of mirrors

CHROMETOPHOBIA
Fear of money

CLINOPHOBIA
Fear of going to bed

ALEKTOROPHOBIA
Fear of chickens

ENTOMOPHOBIA
Fear of insects

FRIGOPHOBIA
Fear of coldness

GERASCOPHOBIA
Fear of growing old

HERPETOPHOBIA
Fear of reptiles

MUSOPHOBIA
Fear of mice

MYRMECOPHOBIA
Fear of ants

OLFACTOPHOBIA
Fear of smells

RHYTIPHOBIA
Fear of getting wrinkles

SCOLECIPHOBIA
Fear of worms

WICCAPHOBIA
Fear of witches

The Golden Arm

Retold by Nicholas Liu

The author Mark Twain used to tell the following story with great care and enthusiasm. He advised that it must be told with the right pause at the end. If the pause is too short, there is no effect; if it is too long, your audience will guess something is up. So at your next slumber party or camp out, see if you can time your pause right and get your friends to yelp and jump out of their seats!

Once upon a time, there was a man who lived alone out on the prairie. The one time he came into town was to find himself a wife, and that he did: a young woman who was fair and kind. Yet even more remarkable was her golden arm—a solid piece of the purest gold—which made her shoulder glitter in the sun and her fingertips sparkle like rays of light. And so, not quite believing his good fortune, he asked her to marry him, she said yes, and they were happily wed.

In time they both grew old, and his wife eventually passed away. The man took her out into the lonely fields, and finding a place he thought she might like by a willow tree—with leaves so old and shaggy, they looked like tiny beards—he buried her. After saying a prayer, he quickly made his way back home as a cold, wintry storm began to settle over the area.

On the night the old man buried his wife, he had himself dinner as usual, read

The Golden Arm

some pages in a book, and tucked himself into bed. Hours later, he was still tossing and turning. But before you think that he was sad because of his poor wife, that wasn't the reason. He couldn't stop thinking about that golden arm. "That arm is worth a fortune!" he said to himself, and now he wondered why he hadn't taken it before he buried her. "She has no need of it now. I'm quite sure she wouldn't have minded."

He reasoned like this with himself long into the night.

Gong . . . gong . . . When the clock began to chime at the stroke of midnight, he felt he could no longer stand it, so he got out of bed, tucked a shovel and lantern under his arm, and forced his way out into the cold sting of the frigid storm. Finding the old willow tree where he had buried his wife, he began digging. When he finally dug her out, he took her arm, and then buried her again. With the beautiful golden arm in his hands at last, he plowed his way back through the thick snow. But as he struggled against the weather, a strange thing happened that made him suddenly stop and listen. *[Make a considerable pause here, look surprised, and act like you're listening for something.]*

He thought he had heard something. "My goodness, what is that?" he said. And he listened as the cold air whipped about him, straining to hear if something was out there in the dark.

The wind howled *[set your teeth together to wail and hiss like the wind]*, "Bssshhh..." and he turned at a sound that seemed to come from the grave itself! It was a voice, barely rising over the moaning wind, but he was quite sure of it now—it was a voice, and it wailed: *"Bssshhh . . . W-h-o . . . g-o-t . . . m-y . . . g-o-l-d-e-n . . . arm? Bssshhhhhhh . . . W-h-o-g-o-t-m-y-g-o-l-d-e-n arm?" [Tremble violently now.]*

Shivering and shaking all over, the man cried out, "Oh, goodness gracious! This can't be!" At that moment, a strong

322

The Golden Arm

gust blew his lantern out, and sleet blew right into his face, making him choke as it went into his mouth and up his nose. Tucking his jacket more tightly about him, he began moving through the knee-deep snow as fast as he could, struggling until every muscle in his body ached—but then soon enough, he heard that voice again, and *[pause]* he realized it was coming after him! *"Bsssssssh . . . W-h-o . . . g-o-t . . . m-y . . . g-o-l-d-e-n . . . arm?"*

Dropping his shovel in panic, he dashed across the frozen field, and when he reached his pasture, he heard it again, even *closer! [Do the wind and voice again.]* With his light out, all he could see was the soft glow of snow all around, but he knew that the sound had come from behind him. When he reached his house, he scrambled up the stairs half running, threw the golden arm under his pillow, jumped into bed, and pulled the covers up to his head. But sure enough, it came—softly at first—and he heard it again! In the quiet of his house,

he listened fearfully *[pause and pretend to be listening along with your audience]* to the slow *pat . . . pat . . . pat . . .* that made its way up the creaking, squeaking stairs. He heard the door latch being lifted, and knew that it was in the room!

With his eyes clamped shut, he shook like the old willow in a breeze, letting out a soft whimper when he knew it was standing by his head. *[Pause.]* And then . . . he felt it bend over him, and he was so frozen stiff from fright that he forgot to breathe. Something *c-o-l-d* had settled close to his head. *[Pause.]*

And then the voice moaned, right by his ear, "W-h-o — g-o-t — m-y — g-o-l-d-e-n arm?" *[Wail this in an accusing manner, and then stare at the most frightened person in the audience. When the pause has become unbearable, reach for that person, jump up and yell:*

"YOU'VE GOT IT!"

323

Ghosts, Ghouls, and Goblins:
HAIR-RAISING TRIVIA

1. What color is a spider's blood?

2. When is the "witching hour," and what is its significance?

3. What do you call a group of witches?

4. Who do Charlie Brown and Linus van Pelt wait for all night in the pumpkin patch?

5. What is the official occupation of a ghoul?

6. Where are the organs of mummies stored?

7. What is Dracula's real name?

8. What shape-shifting creature can always be spotted by the hair on its palms?

9. Why is it dangerous to look directly at a Gorgon?

10. How do vampire bats "suck" the blood of their prey?

1. It's a trick question. A spider's blood is actually colorless and translucent. 2. It is the hour between midnight and one in the morning. It is said that children born during the witching hour posses the ability to see ghosts! 3. A coven. 4. The Great Pumpkin, of course! 5. Grave robber. 6. Ancient Egyptians believed that the bodies of their dead had to be preserved in order that the dead person's soul could reunite with its body in the afterlife. To this end, they even preserved the "essential organs" in jars with lids depicting the heads of the four sons of Horus: the falcon for the intestines, the jackal for the stomach, the baboon for the lungs, and the human for the liver. 7. Prince Vlad Teres, a.k.a Vlad the Impaler. 8. A werewolf. 9. The sight of one of the Gorgons— Medusa, Stheino, and Euryale, the three snake-haired sisters of Greek mythology—was known to turn any mortal into stone. 10. After biting its prey with its incisor teeth, a vampire bat will lap up (like a cat does milk) approximately two tablespoons of blood as its daily meal.

Abracadabra!

*W*ow your friends and impress your family by putting on a magic show! With a little practice, preparation, and bravado, you can make simple illusions and tricks seem impossible. Even if you don't have a magic wand, you'll leave your audience asking, "How did you do that?"

Color ESP

Six or seven different crayons,
small drinking glass

1. Tell the audience that you can "sense" colors. Talk about how colors can reveal things about a person's character.
2. Ask for a volunteer. Have them hold a glass of different colored crayons while you turn your back. Tell the volunteer to choose a crayon and place it in your hand with your back still turned. Ask your volunteer to hide the other colors. When he or she has done so, turn around and keep the selected crayon behind your back.
3. Face the audience and secretly scrape a tiny bit of crayon underneath a fingernail. Then talk about how your volunteer chose a certain color because of his or her mood or personality. Gesture with the hand you used to scrape the crayon. Quickly peek at the color underneath your fingernail and

keep on talking. Then, announce the crayon color and return the crayon to your volunteer using your clean hand. Keep your hands behind your back as you take a bow and remove the crayon scraping.

Magic Paper Clip

Paper clip, glass of water, bar magnet

1. Put the paper clip into the glass of water. The clip should be as close to the edge of the glass as possible.
2. Hide the magnet under the middle finger of your left hand, holding it in place with your thumb. The magnet should be as close to the tip of your finger as possible without it being seen.
3. Place your left hand, palm down, close to the clip and slowly raise your hand up the glass. The clip should rise, following the magnet. Practice this before performing to be sure your audience won't notice the

magnet. You can wave your free hand over the glass and mumble magic words while performing the trick.

Magic Money Clip

Dollar bill, two paper clips

1. Fold the dollar in thirds to form a flat-tened Z. Clip the first and middle section together near the left edge of the dollar. Clip the middle and bottom sections together near the right edge of the dollar.
2. Tell the audience you can magically link the paper clips together without touching them.
3. Tug both ends of the bill to straighten it out. The paper clips will pop off and link together!

Floating Needle

Glass of water, needle, paper napkin, scissors

1. Tell your friends you can make a needle float in a glass of water. Let your friends try first. The needle will sink.
2. Cut out a piece of paper napkin longer than the needle. Place the napkin flat on the water. Lay the needle on top of the napkin.
3. The napkin should sink when wet. If not, push it down carefully with your finger. The needle will stay afloat. Amazing.

Never bend your
head. Always hold
it high. Look the
world straight
in the eye.

—HELEN KELLER

WOMEN OF
POWER

AMINA (1560–1610), Nigerian queen from 1576 to 1610, was a great military leader. Responsible for opening trade routes that helped her African country grow wealthier, she conquered areas to the west and south of her city-state of Zaria and was credited for motivating her city-states to build defensive mud walls to protect them from invaders.

CATHERINE THE GREAT (1729–1796), empress of Russia from 1762 to 1796, was born in Poland and brought many Western ways to her adopted country. Catherine extended Russian territory to include the Crimea and most of Poland. She also sought to improve education, the law, and the ways in which government worked.

CLEOPATRA (69–30 B.C.), queen of Egypt, was famous for her beauty and high style. She had a son by the Roman dictator Julius Caesar. After Caesar's death, she lived with Mark Antony under his protection. Cleopatra and Mark Antony's military forces were later defeated in Greece by Octavius (soon to be the Roman ruler Augustus). Cleopatra was the last pharaoh before the Romans took over Egypt.

ELEANOR OF AQUITAINE (1122–1204), first the queen of France and then queen of England, was the most powerful woman in the twelfth century. Unlike other queens, she traveled often and took great interest in the international politics of the court. Her court was the center of culture, encouraging the art and poetry of the Troubadours. She ruled England during her son's (Richard I) crusade in the Holy Land from 1190 to 1194.

ELIZABETH I (1533–1603), queen of England from 1558 to 1603, made her country a leading power in Europe. She was responsible for restoring Protestantism in England; for the execution of Mary, Queen of Scots; and for defeating the Spanish Armada. This legendary monarch was tolerant of all religions, helped the economy grow, and supported literature and other arts.

ELIZABETH II (b. 1926), queen of England from 1952 to the present, does not have as many powers as the royal monarchs that went before her, but she is still a very popular figure in her country. She is primarily a symbol of the unity and evolution of the British Commonwealth.

INDIRA GANDHI (1917–84), prime minister of India from 1966 to 1977 and from 1980 to 1984, was the daughter of her country's first prime minister, and the first woman ever elected to lead a democracy. During her term as prime minister, Indira adopted a foreign policy of non-alignment, and also took her country into the technological age by launching India's own rocket into space in 1980. Though her time in office was difficult, she was popular enough to have been elected for a second term.

ISABELLA I (1451–1504), queen of Castille from 1474 to 1504 and queen of Aragon from 1479 to 1504, ruled all of Spain with her husband Ferdinand V. In 1479, Isabella united her kingdom of Castille with Ferdinand's kingdom of Aragon, creating the country of Spain. They also succeeded in conquering Granada. In 1492, Isabella approved and financed the trip that would lead to Christopher Columbus's discovery of the New World for the Europeans.

JOAN OF ARC (1412–1431), French military leader, was born a peasant but led the French army successfully against the English in Orleans when she was only seventeen. She also defeated them at Patay. She was canonized as a saint in 1920.

LILIUOKALANI (1838–1917), queen of Hawaii from 1891 to 1893, had the distinction of being its last royal ruler before the United States assumed control. Though she governed the tropical island paradise for only a short while, she tried to restore traditional monarchy to Hawaii. She was declared deposed by the United States and abdicated the throne in 1893. Liliuokalani was known for her musical talents, having composed the famous Hawaiian song "Aloha Oe."

GOLDA MEIR (1898–1978) was prime minister of Israel from 1969 to 1974. Originally an American citizen, Golda Meir immigrated to Palestine in 1921. She was one of the signers of the Israel Declaration of Independence in 1948. As prime minister, she was a tough leader, but she also was known for trying to reduce the conflict between Arabs and Israelis through diplomacy instead of violence.

NEFERTITI, queen of Egypt from 1353 to 1336 B.C. (fourteenth century B.C.), is one of the best-known Egyptian rulers. She was the powerful wife of Akhenaton. Left behind were beautiful sculptures made in her likeness.

MARY ROBINSON (b. 1944), president of Ireland from 1990 to 1997, was the first woman ever elected president in Ireland. Robinson was concerned with improving the health and economic situation of the underprivileged. In 1997, she was appointed United Nations High Commissioner for Human Rights.

MARGARET THATCHER (b. 1925), prime minister of England from 1979 to 1990, was the country's first female to hold this office. Famous for her conservative politics, she was nicknamed the "Iron Lady." She was an advocate for individual freedoms, and was responsible for privatizing Britain's national industries.

TZ'U-HSI (1835–1908), known as the Empress Dowager, ruled China with a strong will, even though technically her 5-year-old son (and later her 3-year-old son) was the emperor. Tz'u-hsi was a conservative leader who eventually grew to favor modernization, including Western innovations like the railroad. She outlawed the use of opium.

VICTORIA (1819–1901), queen of England from 1837 to 1901 and empress of India from 1876 to 1901, ruled for the longest period in English history. During her reign, known as the Victorian age, the country was at its most powerful. Victoria, known for her high standards of morality, brought a renewed popularity to the monarchy.

Little Women (1868) is the story of the four March sisters: Meg, Jo, Beth, and Amy. Set in New England during the American Civil War, this autobiographical novel is a warm story about the transformation from childhood to adulthood. Louisa May Alcott (1832-1888) had an intimate knowledge of the real Little Women, as she modeled them after herself (the fiery, individualistic, imaginative Jo March) and her three sisters, Anna (pretty and proper Meg), Elizabeth (Beth, the gentle darling) and May (the little artist, Amy). Though Alcott took creative liberties with some of the details—for example, it was she who left home to support the war effort, not her father—many of the hardships and triumphs the family experiences were taken directly from her own life. Alcott's novel was so well received that she penned two sequels, Little Men (1871) and Jo's Boys (1886). As the March sisters' story begins, the girls are eagerly planning for Christmas.

"Christmas won't be Christmas without any presents," grumbled Jo, lying on the rug.

"It's so dreadful to be poor!" sighed Meg, looking down at her old dress.

"I don't think it's fair for some girls to have lots of pretty things, and other girls nothing at all," added little Amy, with an injured sniff.

"We've got father and mother, and each other, anyhow," said Beth, contentedly, from her corner.

The four young faces on which the firelight shone brightened at the cheerful words, but darkened again as Jo said sadly,—

"We haven't got father, and shall not have him for a long time." She didn't say "perhaps never," but each silently added it, thinking of father far away, where the fighting was.

Nobody spoke for a minute; then Meg said in an altered tone,—

"You know the reason mother proposed not having any presents this Christmas, was because it's going to be a hard winter for every one; and she thinks we ought not to spend money for pleasure, when our men are suffering so in the army. We can't do much, but we can make our little sacrifices, and ought to do it gladly. But I am afraid I don't"; and Meg shook her head, as she thought regretfully of all the pretty things she wanted.

Little Women

by
Louisa May
Alcott

"But I don't think the little we should spend would do any good. We've each got a dollar, and the army wouldn't be much helped by our giving that. I agree not to expect anything from mother or you, but I do want to buy Undine and Sintram for myself; I've wanted it *so* long," said Jo, who was a bookworm.

"I planned to spend mine in new music," said Beth, with a little sigh, which no one heard but the hearth brush and kettle holder.

"I shall get a nice box of Faber's drawing pencils; I really need them," said Amy, decidedly.

"Mother didn't say anything about our money, and she won't wish us to give up everything. Let's each buy what we want, and have a little fun; I'm sure we grub hard enough to earn it," cried Jo, examining the heels of her boots in a gentle-manly manner.

"I know *I* do,—teaching those dreadful children nearly all day, when I'm longing to enjoy myself at home," began Meg, in the complaining tone again.

"You don't have half such a hard time as I do," said Jo. "How would you like to be shut up for hours with a nervous, fussy old lady, who keeps you trotting, is never satisfied, and worries you till you're ready to fly out of the window or box her ears?"

> **"How would you like to be shut up for hours with a nervous, fussy old lady?"**

"It's naughty to fret,—but I do think washing dishes and keeping things tidy is the worst work in the world. It makes me cross; and my hands get so stiff, I can't practice good a bit." And Beth looked at her rough hands with a sigh that any one could hear that time.

"I don't believe any of you suffer as I do," cried Amy; "for you don't have to go to school with impertinent girls, who plague you if you don't know your lessons, and laugh at your dresses, and label your father if he isn't rich, and insult you when your nose isn't nice."

"If you mean *libel* I'd say so, and not talk about labels, as if pa was a pickle bottle," advised Jo, laughing.

"Don't you wish we had the money papa lost when we were little, Jo?"

"I know what I mean, and you needn't be 'statirical' about it. It's proper to use good words, and improve your *vocabilary*," returned Amy, with dignity.

"Don't peck at one another, children. Don't you wish we had the money papa lost when we were little, Jo? Dear me, how happy and good we'd be, if we had no worries," said Meg, who could remember better times.

"You said the other day you thought we were a deal happier than the King children, for they were fighting and fretting all the time, in spite of their money."

"So I did, Beth. Well, I think we are; for though we do have to work, we make fun for ourselves, and are a pretty jolly set, as Jo would say."

"Jo does use such slang words," observed Amy, with a reproving look at the long figure stretched on the rug. Jo immediately sat up, put her hands in her apron pockets, and began to whistle.

"Don't, Jo; it's so boyish."

"That's why I do it."

"I detest rude, unladylike girls."

"I hate affected, niminy-piminy chits."

"Birds in their little nests agree," sang Beth, the peacemaker, with such a funny face that both sharp voices softened to a laugh, and the "pecking" ended for that time.

> "I hate to think I've got to grow up and be Miss March, and wear long gowns, and look as prim as a China aster."

"Really, girls, you are both to be blamed," said Meg, beginning to lecture in her elder sisterly fashion. "You are old enough to leave off boyish tricks, and behave better, Josephine. It didn't matter so much when you were a little girl; but now you are so tall, and turn up your hair, you should remember that you are a young lady.

"I ain't! and if turning up my hair makes me one, I'll wear it in two tails till I'm twenty," cried Jo, pulling off her net, and shaking down a chestnut mane. "I hate to think I've got to grow up and be Miss March, and wear long gowns, and look as prim as a China aster. It's bad enough to be a girl, anyway, when I like boys' games, and work, and manners. I can't get over my disappointment in not being a boy, and it's worse than ever now, for I'm dying to go and fight with papa, and I can only stay at home and knit like a poky old woman"; and Jo shook the blue army-sock till the needles rattled like castanets, and her ball bounded across the room.

"Poor Jo; it's too bad! But it can't be helped, so you must try to be contented with making your name boyish, and playing brother to us girls," said Beth, stroking the rough head at her knee with a hand that all the dish washing and dusting in the world could not make ungentle in its touch.

"As for you, Amy," continued Meg, "you are altogether too particular and prim. Your airs are funny now, but you'll grow up an affected little goose if you don't take care. I like your nice manners, and refined ways of speaking, when you don't try to be elegant; but your absurd words are as bad a Jo's slang."

"If Jo is a tomboy, and Amy a goose, what am I please?" asked Beth, ready to share the lecture.

"You're a dear, and nothing else," answered Meg, warmly; and no one contradicted her, for the "Mouse" was the pet of the family.

> "If Jo is a tomboy, and Amy a goose, what am I please?" asked Beth, ready to share the lecture.

As young readers like to know "how people look," we will take this moment to give them a little sketch of the four sisters, who sat knitting away in the twilight, while the December snow fell quietly without, and the fire crackled cheerfully within. It was a comfortable old room, though the carpet was faded and the furniture very plain, for a good picture or two hung on the walls, books filled the recesses, chrysanthemums and Christmas roses bloomed in the windows, and a pleasant atmosphere of home-peace pervaded it.

Margaret, the eldest of the four, was sixteen, and very pretty, being plump and fair, with large eyes, plenty of soft brown hair, a sweet mouth, and white hands, of which she was rather vain. Fifteen-year-old Jo was very tall, thin and brown, and reminded one of a colt; for she never seemed to know what to do with her long limbs, which were very much in her way. She had a decided mouth, a comical nose, and sharp gray eyes, which appeared to see everything, and were by turns fierce, funny, or thoughtful. Her long, thick hair was her one beauty; but it was usually bundled into a net, to be out of her way. Round shoulders had Jo, big hands and feet, a fly-away look to her clothes, and the uncomfortable appear-ance of a girl who was rapidly shooting up into a woman, and didn't like it. Elizabeth,—or Beth, as everyone called her,—was a rosy, smooth-haired, bright-eyed girl of thirteen, with a shy manner, a timid voice, and a peaceful expression, which was seldom disturbed. Her father called her "Little Tranquillity," and the name suited her excellently; for she seemed to live in a happy world of her own, only venturing out to met the few whom she trusted and loved. Amy, though the youngest, was a most important person, in her own opinion at least. A regular snow maiden, with blue eyes, and yellow hair curl-ing on her shoulders; pale and slender, and always carrying herself like a young lady mindful of her manners. What the characters of the four sisters were, we will leave to be found out.

Amy, though the youngest, was a most important person, in her own opinion at least.

The clock struck six; and, having swept up the hearth, Beth put a pair of slippers down to warm. Somehow the sight of the old shoes had a good effect upon the girls, for mother was coming, and every one brightened to welcome her. Meg stopped lecturing, and lit the lamp, Amy got out of the easy chair without being asked, and Jo forgot how tired she was as she sat up to hold the slippers nearer to the blaze.

"They are quite worn out; Marmee must have a new pair."

"I thought I'd get her some with my dollar," said Beth.

"No, I shall!" cried Amy.

"I'm the oldest," began Meg, but Jo cut in with a decided—

"I'm the man of the family now papa is away, and I shall provide the slippers, for he told me to take special care of mother while he was gone."

"I'll tell you what we'll do," said Beth; "let's each get her something for Christmas, and not get anything for ourselves."

"That's like you, dear! What will we get?" exclaimed Jo.

Every one thought soberly for a minute; then Meg announced, as if the idea was suggested by the sight of her own pretty hands, "I shall give her a nice pair of gloves."

"Army shoes, best to be had," cried Jo.

"Some handkerchiefs, all hemmed," said Beth.

"I'll get a little bottle of Cologne; she likes it, and it won't cost mush, so I'll have some left to buy something for me," added Amy.

Mother was coming, and every one brightened to welcome her.

New shoes, new shoes,
    Red and pink and blue shoes.
Tell me, what would *you* choose,
    If they'd let us buy?

Buckle shoes, bow shoes,
    Pretty pointy-toe shoes,
Strappy, cappy low shoes;
    Let's have some to try.

Bright shoes, white shoes,
    Dandy-dance-by-night shoes,
Perhaps-a-little-tight shoes,
    Like some? So would I.

But

        Flat shoes, fat shoes,
            Stump-along-like-that shoes,
        Wipe-them-on-the-mat shoes,
            That's the sort they'll buy.

CHOOSING SHOES

By Ffrida Wolfe

Just for Jewels

*I*f you keep losing your rings or finding earrings that don't match, put them on display. You can make a special holder that will keep your favorite charms neat and organized. Then you'll never have to worry about untangling knotted necklaces and bracelets again.

Necklace Tree

plaster of paris, water, small jam jar, chopstick, small tree branch with several sprigs, ribbon

1. Fill the jam jar about halfway full with plaster of paris. Fill the rest of the jar with water and stir with a chopstick until blended.
2. Put the tree branch in the plaster of paris mixture and keep it balanced upright until the plaster hardens.
3. Tie a decorative ribbon around the mouth of the jar. Then "plant" your tree on a dresser or shelf and hang necklaces and bracelets from the branches.

Ring Hanger

Marker, cardboard, scissors, fabric scraps, ribbon, small cup hooks, glue

1. Draw a simple shape on the cardboard, such as a star, heart, or flower and cut it out.
2. Arrange and glue fabric scraps onto the cardboard. Trim the edges with ribbon and glue it in place.
3. When the glue dries, gently screw in the cup hooks to the fabric side of your ring holder.
4. Fold about 8 inches of ribbon in half and glue both ends to the back of the ring holder. Hang on the wall and keep your rings handy on the hooks.

Earring Holder

Clear plastic household cleanser bottle,
marker, scissors, pushpin

1. On each wide side of the bottle, draw a
   basic image, such as a daisy or the outline
   of a cat's head.
2. With scissors, cut the bottle along your
   pattern lines. Leave the bottom of the
   bottle connected to both sides of your
   pattern so that it can stand on its own.
3. Using a pushpin, carefully poke pairs of
   holes on each side of the bottle. You can
   hook your earrings through the holes
   and keep your pairs matched together.

Treasure Tube

Paper towel tube, glue, felt or
decorative paper, ribbon

1. Dab fabric glue along the outside of your
   tube and wrap felt or fabric (cut to fit)
   tightly around the tube. Leave to dry.
2. Run ribbon through the tube leaving
   about 12 inches on either end. Tie both
   ends of ribbon in a bow and hang on
   a hook in your room. Fasten your
   bracelets and watches onto the tube
   and they will be ornamental even
   when not draped on your wrists!!